Lady in Waiting

By Christal Marshall

Design and Layout by Christal Marshall
www.marshallartsstudiophotography.com
www.marshallbook.webs.com
ISBN:

978-1-300-65669-2

To Andrew and Alyvia, my two dreams-come-true.

SYNOPSIS

Priscilla never wanted to be a lady in waiting to the snobbiest Princess in world. She never asked for it. All she wanted to do was to continue to live a humble existence with her family. But after a great tragedy, Priscilla is forced to leave everything she knows for unwanted royal living. She knows that she should be pretty fortunate, but she can never get her little farm out of her mind.

Now the kingdom is in trouble and Priscilla is assigned the undesired task of saving it. Prince Charming can't help, he's tied up somewhere. And there's no magic to break the curse. Love's most powerful kiss can't assist her, (well, maybe a little bit). There's only Priscilla armed with her wit, courage and amazing spirit that will be able to save the Prince and Princess before it's too late.

PROLOGUE

Okay so let's be frank. I hate Prince and Princess stories. I mean I am living in one now and believe me, it's nothing but torture. Fairy Tales always end when the Prince and the Princess fall madly in love and then they get married and all the kingdom rejoices. Then the credits roll and then people go on and live their merry lives.

But that's not real life. Real life is by the time you get to be a Prince or Princess, people have your life already figured out for you and you don't have a choice on anything. Not what you are going to wear, not what you are going to eat or what music you listen to. You don't even have a choice on the most important decisions that you have in your life. For example, who you are you going to marry and where you are going to live.

That's what happened in my kingdom. Our kingdom wasn't doing so hot financially and another kingdom was and some adults got together and thought it would be a good idea to unite the kingdoms in marriage between their son and our kingdom's daughter. Yeah, that plan wasn't really thought out very well.

Last month I went to that horrible and sad wedding and it was pathetic. Two spoiled rich people that have never seen one another before are asked to be husband and wife forever? Let's just say that that wedding would never be at the end of some beautiful fairytale story.

The couple just barely looked at each other the whole time. They were too engrossed in their own selfishness and pride to even enjoy their "most special day of their lives."

The Princess had a dress that I swear took over thirty pounds of swan feathers and twenty pounds of glue to make it all stick together. Her fan was a feathers, her veil was feathers and her gloves had little feather rings on each pinky. But she was sweating profusely. She kept having me dab her dainty forehead with a white handkerchief. She looked so nervous up there on the stage, like a three hundred pound swan that was molting.

The Prince was another kind of bird. He was a peacock. His blue hat had over fifty peacock feathers in it. His blue and teal suit glinted and shone of purple and teal rhinestones. He was a three hundred and fifty pound peacock, even down to his purple and turquoise shoes.

I laughed to myself thinking about how the Prince and Princess shouldn't bother to wear shoes ever because they could never see their feet past their girth, but especially today, their feet were completely hidden amongst the feathers and layers anyways.

"How would I, a poor girl from a poor upbringing, know about such royal fashions and customs?" You might ask. Well, that's a funny story too. I was front and center, a mere foot away from a want-to-be fairy tale. I was a bridesmaid of sorts, because I was a lady in waiting.

1: POTATOES AND CABBAGE

My sleep is awakened once again with a horrible sounding call bell. I slump out of bed, dress quickly and head right for the Princess's chamber, I am thinking the whole time, *I'm going to kill him, I'm going to kill him.*

"Kill who?" You might ask. Well, my father. Well, not literally. I loved my father, I always have, but I really don't like what kind of life he made me get into.

It all started when I was ten years old. My father and mother owned a sheep farm right outside of the palace somewhere. My father was making an honest living selling wool and sheep to the local village. His honesty and character was known throughout our little town. People would come to him just listen to his wisdom.

Even the king found out about my father and came to see our humble farm one day with his daughter. I remember it like it was yesterday. I was feeding slop to our three family pigs and I was wiping sweat from my face and a golden and white carriage pulled up. It had four brown horses with the most regal white hair I had ever seen.

A servant opened the ornate door and lifted his arm to a jeweled hand. The hand stepped out and it was a little girl like me. She had blonde curly hair. But the curls were perfect as if they couldn't move, so perfect that I thought she was an angel. Little did I know that when she grew up, she would be a little ... ahem.

I continued to look and I saw her father, the king, step down. He was handsome and strong. His crown was so shiny that it nearly blinded me as I walked down the path.

My brown sticky hair slimed to the side of my face as I wiped the sweat from my forehead. I was so opposite her, I was so filthy and unkempt next to her porcelain skin and her flushed cheeks.

Even at that age, within five seconds of meeting her, I knew that we would never be friends. As I walked up to bow to her and her father, her face and eyes said it all. She spoke with no words with her expression, "Jealous aren't we?"

Oooh, I just burned with anger then. Of course I was jealous, hasn't every little girl dreamed of being a princess? Hadn't every little girl dreamed of having someone do their hair every morning, dreamed of eating rich foods that aren't the normal potatoes and cabbage? Of course I was jealous, but she didn't have to rub it in. And from that day on, I hated that little girl and vowed to never, ever see her again.

Yeah, like that wish would ever come true. I am getting ready to see this Princess in less than a minute.

The bell rang another time. *I'm going to kill her now!* I thought as I tied an apron around my thin waste. "Miss Pushy Pushy" was now "Mrs. Pushy Pushy" Which made my knick name for her longer and even more annoying to say. *Too much effort to say Mrs. Pushy Pushy,* I thought. *I'll just call her M.P.*

My scowl changed to a half-hearted smile in two seconds flat as I tapped on her chamber door.

"Who is it?" A kind hearted voice asked

"Priscilla," I answered kindly.

Her toned immediately dropped, "What took you so long?" She snarled.

Good morning to you M.P.! I thought. Then I was thrown all her dirty laundry from the day before and a piece of paper for her morning breakfast orders. That's right orders, more than one. The Princess, let's just say, could eat and eat, and eat some more. In fact, I've never seen anyone eat so much. Well, except the Prince I think. And for that reason, and the only reason, they were made for each other.

After putting her orders in and her dirty laundry to the maid's cellar, I went back to my room to finish getting ready for the day. I still needed to brush my hair and snag something for breakfast before having to attend the Princess in her morning activities. She and her new Prince were going to play croquet and watch a horse race afterwards, very exciting, if you ask me. I'd rather watch paint dry then to accompany the Prince and Princess anywhere, especially with Roderick.

Who's Roderick? Well he is the captain of the Prince's body guard. He is definitely built for that position; I'm not going to lie about that. However, he is just as stuck up as the newlyweds and maybe even more so. All he does is work out all the time and wear shirts that emphasize his massive arms. The kingdom knew about him too. All the maids have their own fan club for him.

God, I hate my life. How I wish to be back in the farm with my dad and mom and not have to worry about all this drama.

My mom and dad were wonderful people, very respected. The king's visit really brought my family out of eating potatoes and cabbage for good. Why? Because the king offered my dad a new position: sheep farmer to the king's personal table. Meaning that our sheep wasn't going to be sold for a few farthings at the market, they were personally going to be fed to the King. That meant that our sheep were the best sheep in the kingdom.

The King also took a liking to my father. The King saw the depth of his wisdom and would often visit to share a quiet moment away from the palace pomp and circumstance. I know that the King liked coming as well, because he wanted his daughter to experience a little of her kingdom that she would one day be leading as queen.

Practically speaking, he wanted his daughter to learn to work with many kinds of people. Therefore, he wanted her to be a playmate for me. But it really just ended up as her playing queen and me playing servant day in and day out.

Not really much different as today, I thought as I was brushing my long dark hair. I always had it up in a tight bun for my uniform. But how I wish to hang it wild and free in the wind, riding on my old steed, Marksman.

God, I loved that horse. I loved that horse until it was killed.

I remembered that day too well. He and I were actually out, buying flour and sugar at another town. My mother was home alone, taking care of the animals. I remembered that day because I was so excited to go somewhere with my father, just him and I.

When we came home, all we owned was burned to the ground. My mother's body, we found in the barn, burned to death, next to our cow. It was so vivid to me. I can see my father covering my eyes to this day. Not wanting me to see her this way.

The villagers told us that they saw two men setting fire to the barn and some of them came running to help. By the time they got there with buckets of water, my mother was screaming out and trying to escape the barn. There was no way in. I remember my father weeping when he heard the news.

I never got to say goodbye to her. I always regretted that. I would change everything to see her again, just one last time. I would change everything to have her hold me close one more time, kiss me on my forehead and tell me that I was beautiful. "My little angel" she would say.

After our farm was destroyed, the king heard about the tragedy and came for another visit. He even paid respects to my mother's grave. For that, I respected him. But secretly, deep down in the deepest part of my heart, I hated him and his royal family. I knew that if dad, mom and I kept living our potato and cabbage life, things would have never changed. We still would have been together as a family, me still slopping the pigs and mom still being mom and Marksman still being my best friend.

It all changed that night when the king asked my dad if there was anything that he could do for our family. My dad looked over our smoldering barn and our burned fields and only said one thing,

"That my daughter would be free from this life and have an honest and decent chance at a good upbringing."

I was too young to know what that meant. I was too young to know that the next day a carriage would come and take me to the palace. I was too young to know that that night I was told by the king that my father had died from a broken heart.

I was too young to know what to do.

But now I knew. Ten years had passed. I had gone to the regional palace school, along with all the young rich soon-to-be rulers and leaders. I was tutored next to M.P.'s personal tutor. I learned to read and write and argue with the top young people in the kingdom. Some might say that I am lucky. Others might say that I am living the dream life now.

I don't agree with them. I want my mother and father back. I want my horse back. Secretly, in the deepest, darkest place of my twenty-year-old heart, I want to be free. One day I will find a way to leave this wretched life for a quiet, humble bowl of potatoes and cabbage if I have anything to do with it.

2: PIGS AND CROQUET

The Princess was done with her ten-o'clock second breakfast at the royal dining hall. The Prince was too busy smoothing down his mustache that he didn't even hear M.P. rattle on and on about the beautiful day. He didn’t hear her talking forever about the birds chirping. And he didn’t even pay attention to her complain about her hair not cooperating in tight curls because the humid air was making her sweat like a pig.

I rolled my eyes to myself, getting lost in my thoughts. *Doesn't she know that pigs don't sweat? That's why they roll in the mud! I mean wait, she wouldn't know because she has never lived on a farm before.* I was so bitter in my thoughts that I just sat there smoldering in hatred.

I tried my best to look pleasant and nod at the Princess' many stuffy words, but I just wanted to laugh out loud. This was quite a scene. The Princess was talking to seemingly no one. The Prince was wiping the crumbs off of his dainty mustache and thinly trimmed beard. But he did not see the crumbs under his double chin that was so thick it could have engulfed his face.

And then there was Roderick. In the back with the other body guard members, flexing his muscles and winking at the maids bending down oh so noticeably to dust the bottom of the marble stair well.

I could see Roderick taking a glance at her back side. Disgusted at Roderick and without thinking I said, "Pig."

It was like a pin drop in the room. The two over-sized royals with their many plates of half-eaten food looked at me with shock. Roderick could see that I was looking right at his little show. He glanced away.

I blushed and smiled, "Uhh....we are having pig for lunch, your majesties."

They both smiled and beamed.

The Princess got up as gracefully as a large whale could from the royal table and snapped her fingers for me to reapply her lipstick. "Delightful," she said.

Mrs. Cuire, head chef, glared at me.

I remembered the menu for the week, *Oops; I think we were supposed to have duck today.* I lifted my eyebrows and gave a half smile and shrugged as if to say, "Sorry."

-- -- -- -- -- --

There was a strange air about today. Haggle and Smith could feel it. Something new was in the air and it wasn't their usual stinky feet. It was real. Maybe they'll get a real job today. Not just a stealing chickens kind of job, or a vandalizing the Parrish kind of job, but a real infamous kind of job. The kind of job that would make their father's and grandfather's happy. The kind of job that would make them go down in the books for the sure. Maybe today was their day.

They knew that they were knock heads and clumsy, but at least they tried hard. Their boss only kept them around because they knew that they would do anything. And they knew it. They got assigned some pretty nasty stuff throughout the years, the kind of assignments that they had to throw away their clothes afterwards. Like the time they had to go through the sewer to find evidence that a crooked police officer had flushed down his toilet. And the time they had to put snakes in some rich lady's house. That was pretty gross and scary. But through it all, they only cared about the shiny gold coins they got in the end, so any amount of mice, snakes, sewers, trash, mud, puke, whatever... was worth it.

A little rap at their shack door and a letter was slid under their doorway. They knew it was a job as soon as they got it. The more official the job, the more unofficial the letter from the outside looked. This letter was an advertisement for a circus from the outside and on the inside, there was a handwritten note.

Haggle and Smith read it and their eyes gleamed with greed. They had hit the jack pot.

-- -- -- -- -- --

Croquet was torture. I was trying not to sweat through my royal dress as I held a parasol over the Princess' head for two hours. I kept switching arms because my hands kept falling asleep. And every time I would, I would have to shake my arm a little bit to keep the blood flowing. And every time I would shake, the Princess would glare at me, as if to say, "Do you mind?"

The Prince was doing the usual, paying attention to anything but the Princess. He was interested in joking with his body guards and answering questions from his royal council members. He answered every question, from what to eat next week to foreign affairs.

Because the Prince's kingdom took over our kingdom through their marriage, our poor Princess and her dying father had to deal with being ignored about anything important.

Both kings in fact, were pretty much bed ridden at this point. They were in pretty bad shape and nearly at the point of death. Both kingdoms were sadly waiting for their once strong rulers to pass their legacies on to their heirs. For now, the Council and Prince Gabriel made all the major decisions.

The Princess was in her own little world of course. She was signing, actually singing to the birds or whatever creatures she could imagine in her head. Well, I wouldn't call it singing, I would say scaring. I guess in her own mind, she was a wonderful singer, but to the rest of us, it was torture. I mean, don't get me wrong. I'm no opera performer myself. In fact I can literally only carry a tune in a bucket, but at least I don't try to sing beyond my capacity.

After my arm fell asleep for the seventh time and my other arm was tired of waving a fan at M.P.'s golden locks that had now deflated to a limp curl, it was finally time to go to lunch. My afternoon wasn't over yet, I still had the pleasure of going to lunch and then the horse race.

Lunch, oh yeah we are having duck. I love duck, one of the only meals that I'll eat at this place. *Oh wait, crud. Never mind, we are having pig. Thanks to my big, fat mouth.*

My big fat mouth is the reason that I know I would never make a good Princess. I mean I am so sarcastic, mean-hearted, and full of schemes. I am definitely not the fairy-tale type of Princess that you read about. But obviously we already know that real fairy-tales won't come true, so I guess in my own little world, I could be the Princess of something.

Lunch of ham and potatoes au gratin with a side of spinach and goat cheese was secretly very tasty. I even went up to the cooks and praised them for their creativity.

Mrs. Cuire had taken a liking to me since I came to the palace as a ten year old. She winked at me and said, “Priscilla Louise Agneu,” and then she went to spank me with her wooden spoon. She laughed a hearty laugh, “How could I be mad at you? I’ve taken care of you ever since you came here.” She turned to stir her soup and taste it. “Lucky for you, a new farmer moved into town today that had lots of pigs to sell at a good price.”

She added a little oregano to the broth, “He was pretty handsome you know.”

I had drifted off, looking at Roderick flirting with another maid. Even though he was full of himself sometimes, okay, all the time, I know I’ve seen a kinder side of him, the kinder side that he was too afraid to share with anyone. All he seemed to care about was a handsome facade. But I knew he had a good heart. Like the time that he helped the coachmen wash off the horses and the time that the wheel broke in the carriage and he personally fixed it.

I also knew his deepest secret and he knew that I knew. But for some reason he never threatened me to not tell. It was like he secretly trusted me with it. And I liked our far-away little no-relationship that we had. No feelings, no drama, just knowing that we secretly trusted one another.

I remember that night very distinctly. I was taking out the trash and I saw through the rain, a figure at the back gate. Roderick was passing some food to the beggar. Technically I knew it was stealing and technically I could report Roderick. But I knew that really deep down, giving some our rich food away from the fat bellies of the royals and passing it on to someone that really needed it wasn't all that bad. He saw me watching him, he looked down, ashamed, but that night, I never asked him about it or questioned him.

I drifted back to reality. All I heard was "He was pretty handsome you know." I thought Mrs. Cuire was talking about Roderick.

I scoffed, "No. He knows that he's handsome. And for that, I don't respect him." Which was partially true.

Mrs. Cuire laughed and deep belly laugh. "Priscilla, I was talking about the pig farmer I met today. He was about your age." She broke her speech and laughed some more. "But I can obviously see that you have your eyes on someone else."

I put my hands up in defense. "No way. I am definitely not a member of his fan club. Oh no, not me."

Mrs. Cuire looked at me with that slanty lip face that she always did when she knew that I was lying and said nothing, which said it all.

3: A FAMILY OF THREE

Áron Sika was feeling pretty good about himself. He had just moved into town and he had already gotten work from the king's table. His luck was beginning to change. He never had so much luck before. His father had just passed and left him the farm and all the livestock. Famine hit his little town and people were starting to leave in all directions. One particular village, Castlegate, was rumored to have good fortune. So he decided to move his livelihood closer to the castle and try his luck at a new place.

Now an orphan and feeling alone, Áron needed to provide with his two younger sisters and their small farm. He could do it, he knew. He had been doing it know for five years or so while dad was on-and-off sick. At twenty five, he knew that this was where he needed to be.

As he and his sisters entered the new town, herding their pigs and cows and sheep, he saw the beautiful white palace on the horizon. He loved his life of the ordinary; he loved feeling like he was close to his animals and nature, but what he wouldn't give for a warm bath in that palace. He didn't think he could live there for good, not enough things to do. He had been a hard worker all his life, but for one night, just one night, that would be good enough.

Emmi, twenty and Kai, sixteen were also amazed at the beautiful site. They were farm girls through and through, but always dreamed of seeing a palace or a royal, or both.

Emmi, was especially hard working and loved the county life, but secretly, deep down, she wished to live a fairytale. She would never let on to her younger, more romantic sister, who would daydream all the time about meeting a "Prince Charming." Emmi was just a realist. She knew hard work was the only way to get anywhere in life, hard work and perseverance.

Kai was just giddy thinking about the Prince. She had heard that he had just gotten married. She sounded heartbroken that a prince, "Her Prince," apparently had gotten himself married. But being a girl with romantic pursuits, she understood that there were always other princes.

She then began to prattle on and on about every detail that she had heard about. "The flowers were imported from France. The Champagne from Italy, The cake from Barcelona..."

Emmi, a little more grounded. "Kai, do you think that a cake would be imported from Spain, that's like a million miles away? By the time it got here, it wouldn't be fit to eat!"

Kai shrugged, "I guess so but it would be a cool thing if it really did happen."

Áron got lost in his thoughts as they came to some farm land that looked as it had been abandoned for years. After asking some of the locals about the land, they said, "No one's been there for years. People think it's haunted. The only heir is long gone by now."

Áron laughed, "Haunted? By what?"

The butcher said, "By the woman of the house, they say. They say she was burned alive with her dairy cow."

Áron looked serious at first and then looked at the old butcher's blushed face. Then they both laughed a hearty laugh.

That afternoon they made it to the old farm. There was a lot of work to be done. They first had to make a house. Emmi and Kai went around the village asking for help chopping logs and building their cabin. Their pretty blue eyes were definitely a winner for the butcher's son, the baker's son and the Thatcher's sons. More people came from the village, until there was a house raising get-together, complete with home cooked meals by the local women.

As luck would have it, a servant and a large woman came to the gate of Áron's field as they were all eating. The servant was dressed in royal robes and the cook's apron looked fresh and new, unlike the local baker's and wine presser's.

He walked up to the strangers and extended a hand to both. The strangers were surprised by his friendliness. They told him that they were from the palace and in desperate need of pigs.

"Well, you both are in luck," Áron said confidently.

"We just happened to move into town today and we just happen to have some pretty fine pigs."

Áron sold his two finest pigs that day and made double what he would have made elsewhere. The townspeople had all helped to support and feed their family and he had made good money! Wow, what a great first day!

The next day, ten or so more young people came to help the Sika family. The woman and children brought over baked goods and the fathers came with their tools. It was definitely a community event.

At the end of the week, after many shifts of young men and old men who came to help, their little two room house was soon taking shape. Áron was pleased with his acceptance in the community at large and invited all to a pig roast the following night.

Life couldn't get any better.

Well, it could have if he had someone to share it with. That's what he always wanted. A quiet life with someone to love him and love what he does.

-- -- -- -- -- --

Emmi Sika was a fiery blonde with fiery blue eyes. She loved a good intrigue and also the quietness of the farm life. But secretly, passionately, she yearned for an adventure. At least one. An adventure so memorable that she would have to write it down and share it because it would be stuff of legend.

At twenty years old now, she was getting restless. She had taken care of her sister Kai and the family's farm as long as she could remember. Mom died giving birth to Kai, so she was the mother of the household and she knew it. She would never abandon her family, but she wished for something new.

Ever since her brother decided to move them from their old town of Ravenscrook to here in Castlegate, she knew that something new was coming her way. She could feel it. It was in the air, like the wafting of her next door neighbor's bakery. Their son was about her age. Gorgeous green eyes too. Maybe she could get used to this place.

-- -- -- -- -- --

The horse race was uneventful to me. I mean if you count uneventful as a sticky, hot day with loud horses galloping down a dirt path, pooping at the finish line and flies swarming in your face, then yes it was uneventful.

I couldn't help but watch Roderick. He was really into horses and this whole race horse thing. *Definitely a guy thing.* I thought to myself. The Princess looked just as unexcited as me. M.P. was too busy ordering me to fan the flies away from her face to really enjoy the company of her new groom.

I looked over to the back of the small arena. The Council was talking as usual. The Council, you know all the old guys that make the real decisions in our kingdom. The royalty has a say, but it's really the Council that knows all the ins and outs. I'm totally oblivious to what's going on. That's the truth. I just know when to curtsey, when to smile, when to get M.P.'s hair brush and when to hide from being called.

That's kind of a sucky life. I admit. No future, no dreams, no vision. But what am I supposed to do? I have food on the table, I have my maids and cooks as friends and family, I have a steady job, I have a roof over my head, I'm warm at night... I guess I have no right to complain.

What would I do if I left? I would have to find a job and a house to live in. But what are my skills? Being a maid, a housekeeper and an assistant. I can read and write, but I have no further job skills than that. So if I did leave, I would have to find a job as a servant and live with a family. So I wouldn't really be going from good to greater.

I do know what to do on a farm though, but that job doesn't really pay well. I mean what am I supposed to do, go to some farm and knock on their door and say, "So I was just running away from the palace from being the lady in waiting to our Princess, because I got tired of the posh palace life and the great food every day, so I was wondering if you were hiring a pig slop girl?" I knew I would totally be laughed out of town.

I realize that millions of girls would kill to have my job. But for some reason, my nice paying job with my nice clothes just isn't cutting it for me. I guess I ultimately stick with it because it's what my father would want for me. I mean, he's the one that made the King basically raise me in the palace to have the nice life that he could never give our family.

I guess maybe I am just getting restless. Restless for what? I am not sure, just a change or something new.

-- -- -- -- -- --

Roderick Braun was living the high life. He was body guard to Prince Gabriel and infamous for his good looks and suave personality. He had it all on the outside. He could see Priscilla down there with Princess Isabella. She was having a rough time. The flies were torturing them. He didn't mind the flies, they didn't really like him anyway, they usually liked flowery smells.

Priscilla was waiving a fan, trying to keep the flies out of the Princess' hair. She could totally quit and leave this life. But she never complained and never seemed sullen or angry. He had to admit that Priscilla was scrappy and he liked that about her. She took whatever crap that the Princess gave to her and took it while keeping a smile. He respected that.

He definitely felt sorry for her though. She had no family. He knew that she was an orphan and that she had lost everything in a fire when she was ten. But he was jealous of her in one way, better to have no family, but good memories, then a family that you were constantly trying to run away from.

He knew that he had had a similar story. He was actually adopted by the Prince's tutors at the age of ten and was allowed to grow up in the palace. He attended the regional royal school to learn from the best teachers in the land. This was the school where all the leaders of the different countries and kingdoms sent their future leaders and debutants. He was very privileged to go and was of course a top student with both the teacher's and the ladies.

The King was the one who first saw his potential. He would never forget the king's kindness towards him, and with that he vowed his life to protecting his son, not matter what it took.

Roderick always wanted to be a better man than his father or uncles were, hence the constant pull to be stronger, smarter and more handsome then they were. His relatives were thieves. They knew about his new employment in the castle and used it to their full advantage.

"Roderick," they would smirk at him, "Could a good ol' nephew slip some of tonight's dinner threw the gate for a poor uncle and his family?" They would ask weekly questions like this. First it was food, and then it was small mementos of the palace: a tassel from the curtain, a piece of log from the fire, their requests grew more extravagant as the years progressed.

But he was trapped. He knew that if didn't appease his relatives they would find a way to get inside the castle and blackmail the royals. Those were just the kind of scum his family were, the lowliest of it too.

He looked at Priscilla's dark brown eyes. They were deep brown, like the color of honey. She knew his secret. He didn't really know how much, but she knew something was going on with him, but she would never tell what.

He remembered that rainy and cold night. One of his uncles had come over to get some scraps. Roderick was trying to sneak out of the castle without being noticed. But it was too late. Priscilla was taking out the trash when she noticed him passing food through the back fence. But she never asked about it and never brought it up to him. And for that he respected her even more.

He could never bring himself to tell her his back story. He was much too guarded for that. He knew that if he did, he would have to let her know eventually the kind of life that he had come from. And he could never forgive himself for that.

-- -- -- -- -- --

The race was done, finally. I helped to get M.P. and all the twenty five layers of her dress in the carriage without looking as though it was the heaviest thing I have ever lifted. Even though it really was.

The Prince came in after us, shifting the weight of the carriage significantly to his side. Roderick climbed on top with another body guard and they balanced it on my side. And we were off. Well, I guess you could say we were off. It felt though as if we were only going five miles an hour since our total weight on the carriage was over 1,000 pounds collectively. I think our palace horses are especially breed to carry this type of weight. *Poor Horses.*

The Prince broke the awkward silence of the sticky carriage ride by saying, "I thought we could drive through the village on our way back to the castle."

M.P. didn't even look up from fixing her hair. She snarled at me to fan faster and faster. The sweat was pouring down my back now. You would think that the royal carriages would have some type of fan system or something.

The Prince took the silence as a "Yes." So he told the driver to take the scenic route.

This detour was not really out of the ordinary for the royals. About once a month, the Council required them to visit and wave like a parade through the village so that the people could fawn over them and "know" their royals.

Personally I didn't really understand how a carriage ride and waving was supposed to make a better kingdom when people needed food and homes. But I am not one to argue with the Council.

We came over the hill and the village opened up before us. This seemed like what I always dreamt of my home looking like. I honestly didn't know specifically where I grew up. I was only ten when I left my home an orphan. All my memories are little bits and pieces with faded blurs.

I passed by a bakery and a butcher shop, everything was rustic and quaint, like it was out of a picture book. I started to day dream. I dreamed of growing my own garden, just like my mom used to do. I wished this place to be my home in the future, far away from the palace and close enough to everything I needed.

I could smell the wafting of baguettes and rolls in the late afternoon air. The butcher shop was alive with sparks of red and yellow fire. Children saw us and waved. They ran to tell their parents. Soon there was a small crowd forming.

I could tell that the Prince was making mental notes of the town. He was looking at the condition of the homes, the streets and the businesses. He looked genuinely concerned, like he actually cared for the people. Sometimes all I saw was a pompous blue peacock. But I saw a small spark, a spark of a leader that wanted to be a good leader. It was rare to see the Prince in a serious mood.

I was making mental notes of the streets as well; they were definitely bumpy for our massive carriage. There was mud everywhere and mysterious holes that you didn't know you were going to ride over until you dropped into one.

After one such particular bump, I knew that our wooden wheels couldn't take the weight much longer. And just as fate would have it we slipped into one such deep hole that we started to tip.

The royals' faces were hilarious to watch, going from stoic to scared in t-minus ten seconds. If we weren't tipping so rapidly into what looked like the biggest puddle of mud that I've ever seen, then I would be laughing out loud right now.

The splash that we heard was the biggest, loudest splash of mud coming our way that we ever heard. The mud slushed and slipped into our carriage, like a big royal brown, sticky, gross mess.

No one was hurt, but I couldn't help but laugh at the irony of where we were. We were standing in front of pig farm and we ourselves were huge pigs covered from head to toe in mud.

4: HELP IN ON THE WAY

Roderick held out his hand to me first to get me out of the carriage. I was relieved because M.P. was squished against me like a sardine. The Prince helped his wife out of the carriage. They were quite the couple. Their royal robes covered in mud. Their painted faces and powdered hair pieces drooping and dripping with wet. I thought this was a very comical sight indeed, but of course I had to stifle my laughs.

And that's when I realized that being royal and acting royal is two very different things. The royals' reaction was just as I had expected: childish and shallow.

First M.P. cried about her hair and dress getting messed up. And the Prince started yelling at the driver. Roderick and I just looked at each other as if to say, "What do we do now?"

A small crowd had gathered to see us be humiliated. The children were shushed by their parents not to laugh or make any mocking noises. Roderick sent the drivers to run to the castle to get another carriage. But by that time it would be night time. The castle was a good five to ten miles away. And I knew that the drivers were not in the best of shape.

While Roderick and I were standing and thinking about what we needed to do, a farmer got our attention. He took off his hat and bowed low. It was the most regal bow that I ever seen. His hair was blonde and ruddy. His clothes were muddy as well, but not a crude way. Just a way to say, "I'm a hard worker."

He spoke up, his voice was strong. "Your majesties."

The royals stopped their bickering and looked at the farmer. They looked annoyed and perturbed. He looked caring and humble.

The farmer continued, "I can help put your carriage back up and fix the wheel if you all would like."

The farmer signaled to a pretty blonde woman running toward him. The woman came near and the farmer whispered something in her ear and pointed to the village. The woman nodded and ran toward the baker's shop.

"The village is going to help us." The farmer smiled a beautiful soft smile.

I did a little flip in my heart, but then remembering the woman that had come with the beautiful blonde hair, I guarded myself. *Of course, it's always the nice guys that get married first.*

About ten minutes later, a group of young men came with ropes, horses and donkeys. Slowly and methodically they pulled the carriage from the muck and put in back right side up. The blacksmith and the farmer started hammering and fixing the wheel of the huge carriage.

The farmer was very concentrated the whole time, directing people, asking for tools and sending people to gather the things that were needed. Every hand helped, every hammer swung, every rope pulled, every hand got dirty. Even Roderick jumped in.

The blonde woman and another blonde girl put blankets around the two royals and my shoulders. The bickering of the royals stopped and only silence remained.

We were all humbled by the ingenuity and the kindness of the village people.

I was glad for the blanket, because the night air was coming in a little by little with the dusk of the sky. M.P. and the Prince looked like wet and sad dogs, whimpering in self-pity. I needed a job to do to help them as well, so I got up and looked for the blonde women.

I couldn't find them around, so I walked up to the farmer who was putting the finishing touches on the wheel.

I bent low to the ground and watch him work under the carriage, hammering and wiping sweat from his brow. I spoke in a voice gentile and kind, "Excuse me sir, could I trouble you for some water for the Prince and Princess?"

He was startled and arose quickly and bumped his head on the carriage. He bowed awkwardly, "Yes ma'am. Follow me please."

He opened his gate to me as we walked to the farm house. The sunset was beautiful. If I wasn't cold and in covered in mud, then I would have thought this was a beautiful moment to watch unfold.

He opened his small home to me and I stepped inside. There was a small fire in the fireplace. The tall blonde woman was at the sink washing potatoes and cabbage. I almost cried. It was like being home again. The smell of the soup on the fire, the wood walls and small rocking chair near the mantel, it all was like a wash of memories.

The farmer could see that I had stopped walking and was looking around."My humblest apologies m'lady for the poor house."

I touched his arm, "No. It's perfect. I actually grew up in a village like this one before everything was taken away from me. It's like being home here."

He looked at me, "What did you parents do?"

I looked up at him, "They were sheep farmers."

"Where are they now?"

I looked down, "They're gone. They died when I was little."

He looked embarrassed, "I'm so sorry."

There was awkward silence between us. The tall blonde woman was chopping carrots and we heard the *crunch crunch* of the knife. She threw the orange bits into a large pot.

I answered the question that his mind was probably thinking, "If you wondering how I got to work with the Princess, it's kind of a long story."

He laughed, "I was kind of curious myself. It's rare to meet someone that works in the palace. I am but a humble sheep farmer."

I smiled, "My father's dying wish was to have me be raised in the palace so that I could have a chance at a better life than my family. The king and my father were friends when I was little. The King is a good man. He respected my father, and for that I respect the King and vowed to serve his daughter."

The farmer handed me some cups, "Do you like living at the palace?"

I knew that I shouldn't complain but honesty is always my strongest characteristic. "Well, no, to be honest. I am the lady in waiting to M.P...." I was terribly embarrassed that I let my personal nickname come out of my big mouth. I corrected myself, “I mean, the Princess.” I blushed “I have to admit it’s not always the most fun work.”

He laughed, “M.P.? What does that mean?”

I shooshed him and whispered in a conspiring tone, “Don’t tell anyone, because it would be very disrespectful if anyone knew that I thought this way.”

He laughed and crossed his heart, “Cross my heart.”

I said embarrassed, “M.P. means, Mrs. Pushy Pushy.”

Both the blonde at the sink and the farmer laughed. Another blonde young lady opened up her door to peek out and laugh too.

The farmer put on his hat again and said, “I know that I wasn’t raised in the palace school and I am just a poor farmer, but Mrs. Pushy Pushy really should be called M.P.P.”

I rolled my eyes, “I know,” I huffed and rolled my eyes, “But since she got married and became a Mrs, it’s just a pain to have a knick name longer than the real name.”

I was given three cups of water. I knew that Roderick would probably want some. I balanced three cups on a tray. More like juggling three cups on a little tray, I am not the most graceful servant. I nodded to the man and the two women, “I’m Priscilla by the way. Thank you all so much for your kindness.”

The farmer nodded back and bowed his head, “I’m Áron,” He pointed to the woman at the sink, “This is my sister Emmi” then he pointed to the teenager in the doorway, “And this is my other little sister, Kai.”

Kai opened the door all the way, "Áron, I'm not little any more, how many times do I have to tell you that?"

I nodded my head, and laughed, missing sibling rivalries that I never had the chance to participate in. I smiled at everyone, "Nice to meet you all. It's been wonderful to see you all serve the royals so kindly."

Áron could see that I was struggling with the tray and he offered to take it for me. His hands were strong and hard working. I liked him immediately. Áron led me out as he put another hammer in the loop of his work pants.

The evening sun was setting and his blonde hair blew slightly in the wind, his shoulders were strong and tall. He balanced the tray and courteously opened his gate to me and nodded.

He then spoke my name and made it sound so beautiful. "Priscilla, I'm not usually this forward."

I could hear his voice nervously faltering as he continued. "I know we just met, but you make me laugh. There's hasn't been many women that have really made this much impression on me."

I hoped that it was definitely a good impression. Personally I thought I was always an ungraceful twit when it came to conversations with the opposite sex, hence my embarrassingly dateless love life. I had received a *few* courting proposals, but only from the garbage men and some random guy in the dungeon. Does that count? I didn't think so. But I figured, if a guy can't appreciate me for me, than he isn't worth my time.

Áron's lips came close to my ear; he tickled it as he said, "Is there any way for us to see each other again?"

I knew that he probably didn't want his village buddies to hear his proposal, unlike Roderick's style of yelling to beautiful girls, "Hey gorgeous, how about lunch with me this Thursday? I'll bring the champagne?" And surprisingly enough, Roderick was a usual nine times out of ten success rate in the "yes" department.

In contrast, Áron was shy, humble, hard working. It was like he didn't usually ask out girls. It was like when he asked me, it was special, like I was the only one that he had ever asked. I immediately liked that about him but I was taken aback. I had just met him too. I liked him, I thought he was handsome and well-mannered, but I didn't know much about him.

"Umm..." I mumbled and I looked around. Of course my elegant tongue would be the first to charm him.

Áron looked down embarrassed, "you of course are already seeing someone." He nodded toward Roderick as he was helping the butcher's son with the carriage.

I laughed hysterically. The men at the wagon looked up. Roderick looked to see if it were him that I was laughing at. I hushed my laughing, "Oh no, definitely not Roderick and I..." and I trailed off thinking of the humor and the irony our pair would be. Handsome and the Least. Oh that would be hilarious to see us together. His suave personality and totally buff arms walking hand in hand down some beautiful garden path and then I trip on some rock and land in the mud face first, how romantic.

We both laughed until the awkwardness set in again. I tried to put on my girly face, "I think we can arrange another meeting." But really my girl face was more like a half fish face with fluttering eye lashes.

He laughed at my impersonation of some socially graceful dame fanning myself with an invisible bejeweled fan. Then I turned and walked toward the Prince and M.P. and looked back at Áron to see if he was looking at me. He was and he was smiling.

-- -- -- -- -- --

Prince Gabriel sat in the mud puddle looking at his bride of one month. Even though she was drenched from head to toe and her usual pristine royal robes were sopping wet, she was quiet. In the silence the Prince admired her.

He took a moment to look at his life in this mud puddle. All his accolades and medals seemed so shallow in this puddle. He looked at his bride; her royal robes were dripping and limp. He knew that even though he wanted to ignore the fact that they were very similar, he knew it to be true. They were both pretty self-centered, especially him. They both had reacted selfishly to their drivers and their servants. He regretted his actions.

When was the last time that he'd actually had a conversation with her? He couldn't remember. They met days before their wedding. She was stunning on their wedding day but he would never let it get to him. He was trying to be a leader of this united kingdom and he didn't want to have his feelings get in the way. He needed to be focused.

He knew that the Council and the people were counting on him to fix their problems. His father was at the end of his life. Gabriel could see in his mind eye, his father, surrounded by no one, lying alone in his massive room, just waiting for death to come. It was a sad ending to his father's great story. Gabriel hoped to bring honor to his father and the kingdom that he had come to lead.

The first step to a great rule was to change his attitude. His tutor would always tell him, "Leaders aren't born great leaders; they are forged by the fires of time and tribulation."

As a young man, he never knew what that meant, but Gabriel knew now. He needed to be a leader in the tough times in order to be a good leader in the best of times.

-- -- -- -- -- --

Emmi was making dinner. She was suspicious of the brown-haired girl at first. But after hearing her talk to Áron in the cottage about her life working for the Princess, Emmi liked her immediately. She was real. Not stuck up or too proud to do work. She had come from humble beginnings and was honoring her family by working in the palace.

Emmi could hear the soup come to a steady boil. She leaned down to smell her cabbage soup percolating with onion, oregano and potato. She enjoyed cooking and bringing something inanimate to life.

She thought of her brother and Priscilla. She could see their future together. She looked back at her life, mostly focused on raising Kai. Now in this new place, maybe Emmi could think about herself for a change.

She looked outside at the men helping with the carriage. The baker's son was there, swinging a hammer with his hefty arms. In fact, the baker's son had winked at her today as he saw her on the way to help the poor Prince and Princess. He was kind of cute, she had to admit. But she knew that her standards were really high. She would have to get to know him first before making any rash decisions.

She usually preferred men that had hands and knew what to do with them. She liked the way her father's hands used to feel, hard working and worn, like an old leather coat. Her father was also a brave man, protecting the family from many droughts and storms. She could see him covering the horses and the cattle with the blankets when it turned cold. He was so conscientious and kind. Emmi wanted to find a man like that.

She glanced out her cottage window. Most of the people had left for the evening and to finish their work before the sunset. But there were three young men still out there, the baker's son, her brother and a dark haired muscular guy. She couldn't deny that he was handsome. He had even looked her way one to two times. He was definitely mysterious, she knew that much. And she admired the way that he was working, knee deep in dirt and mud to fix the wheel.

She wasn't one to fall for a handsome face though. She had seen too many shallow men with pretty faces. She was looking for a man with a deep spirit.

She looked out the window again, the baker's son had given up the fight and only Áron and the handsome man remained. They were the only two that could handle this hard task.

She smelled the soup again. It was perfect and bubbling hot. *Maybe this soup would be just the thing to help them out.* She thought to herself as she ladled the broth into seven bowls. She included the royals and their servant girl. *What was her name again?* Priscilla.

-- -- -- -- -- --

Roderick looked up and wiped sweat off of his brow. The evening was coming in and he was famished. He smelled something wonderful. Not like the fancy meals of the castle, but something made from a home-cooked fire. Coming out of Áron's cottage was the beautiful blonde young lady with bowls of something hot and steamy. Roderick always had a weakness for blondes, especially ones that could cook. But he was hesitant. Áron and she looked like kin, but it was really hard to tell sometimes. He couldn't be too careful.

He could tell that she was balancing seven bowls on an old tray. He ran up to help.

She smiled at him and handed him two bowls and said, "Thank you so much."

Roderick could smell the hot steaming soup. His stomach was growling now ferociously.

"It smells wonderful." Roderick begin as he led her down to path.

"It was my mother's favorite soup to make," said the blonde.

Roderick did the math of the people outside in his head. He knew there were seven, but he wanted a way to keep the conversation going, "Why seven bowls?"

The blonde laughed, "My brother, you, me, my sister, Priscilla and the Prince and Princess."

Roderick was pleased, *just the answer I was looking for. Áron's sister. Well, Áron, don't mind if I do.*

5: A PLOT

Princess Isabella was humbled by the young lady who was bringing soup for everyone, while she was waiting for the carriage to get fixed. Compared to the common everyday townspeople she knew that she looked ridiculous. Not only was she still in her soiled royal dress, but her attitude was sullen and dirty as her exterior.

She wished that she could be as humble as her servants or as flexible as Priscilla. How she wished sometimes that she was just an everyday person. But she honestly had never been given a chance to be one, nor taught how to be one.

Her mother, who died when she was only a little girl, never showed her the way to act. All of Isabella's memories of her mother were of a beautiful lady that was constantly putting on makeup and trying on dresses. Isabella honestly couldn't remember having a real conversation with her about anything truly important.

Her father tried to raise her as much as he could, but all the Princess' governesses had the most impact on her life. They taught her how to walk, how to talk, how to act as a princess could. They created the monster and Isabella had to act like the creature that they had made.

Isabella looked around at her village. They were good people, hardworking and kind. She respected her town's people. How she wished her palace was filled with just a handful of them. Most of her staff seemed cross or uptight, kind of like her actually. If only some people could see the real her, the her that was waiting to come out, then she knew that the palace, and the kingdom would be a much nicer place.

She wanted to repay these people somehow, give them some kind of thank you gift for their deeds. *Maybe a thousand pieces of gold? No. Too extravagant. Maybe a ball in their honor? Maybe, it'll will give me a chance to wear my new shoes. Gosh, listen to me. I am completely self-centered.*

She couldn't even think about others for one minute before her old self wanted to creep in and steal the show. How she needed to change and fast.

Everyone gathered to sit down outside. There were the two blondes and their brother, the farmer. Roderick, Priscilla and Prince Gabriel also came near to eat the warm soup together.

The Princess cleared her throat and spoke up in the silence. Come to think of it, it was the first time that she could remember that she had anything of worth to really say in a long time.

"I know personally, I wanted to thank you all for helping us today." She looked down humbly at her soup.

Gabriel spoke up as well, "I agree with the Princess, I mean... my wife..." It was like saying "wife" was a little awkward for him still.

Isabella continued, "What can we do for you family to say 'thank you?'"

The small teenager spoke up first, "Just to see the palace and sleep in a royal bed would be the greatest dream ever." She looked towards the castle in the moonlight, her eyes shining with wonder.

The older young lady with the blonde hair glared at her. She definitely didn't look happy that her sister spoke up.

Gabriel looked at Isabella and they shrugged, "What a wonderful idea," they both said.

The Prince spoke alone, "You all will be our personal guests one evening for dinner and for the night."

Isabella beamed and said, "We'll have a party in your honor."

The young farmer, Áron, butted in, "That's not necessary, your highness."

The blonde teenager glared at him. Isabella laughed, "It would be our honor to host you that night."

The teenager squealed. Even the farmer looked happy. Priscilla beamed.

-- -- -- -- -- --

Áron and his family were getting geared up to go to the palace in a week. The Princess had announced that their stay would be a kingdom-wide event: music, dancing, singing, food , and extravagant costumes. Emmi and Kai were in a frenzy. They were combing their hair, pinching their cheeks and ironing their dresses to prepare. It was going to be a night that they would never forget. The night that they would visit the castle, dance to music, see fantastic costumes and stay in a royal bed.

Áron was not only very excited about the royal sized bath tub, but about seeing someone very special. Áron's long legs had yearned to stretch out and relax with warm bubbles. But he was even more excited to see the beautiful Priscilla. Hopefully, if he was lucky, he could steal her for a dance.

Kai was literally jumping up and down at the thought of a royal ball. "What will we wear?" She kept asking Emmi.

Emmi, who always was sound of mind and usually didn't care what other people thought, was a little nervous about that night. "I don't know Kai, perhaps we should make our own dresses." was her only answer.

-- -- -- -- -- --

My stomach is in knots. It was my first ball. Well, not technically. I've been to balls all the time. But I was only the help getting the Princess ready in her seventeen layers and her fifteen layers of makeup. This ball I could actually attend as a guest. I was also nervous because Áron was going to be there. Even if he showed up in old work boots and a farmer shirt, he would still look so handsome.

It seemed like everyone after our little adventure had changed, including M.P. She was kinder, sweeter, and even said "Thank you" one time. I nearly fell over. She had definitely changed for the better and hopefully on a more permanent basis. I am suspicious though. I keep thinking that beneath that sweet exterior is a ferocious lion just waiting to jump out. But to my surprise, no lion jumps out, just more sweetness.

Today, the maids brought in new clean pillows for the Princess. They forgot to bring the M.P.'s favorite flowers. Usually M.P. expects lavender flowers tied up with a purple ribbon to decorate her pillows. And usually she gives them a tongue lashing if they forget, but she didn't complain or have a hissy fit today. She just ignored the missing flowers and said instead, "Lovely day today isn't it ladies?" I saw their faces. It was like they were bracing themselves for the worst. But nothing happened. They looked as if they would fall over too.

I definitely have to think about changing M.P.'s nickname to something a little less degrading. Maybe I'll call her "The Princess." I don't know, too soon for that. She will really have to prove herself to me first. *Hmm... I 'll really have to think about this.*

Roderick even told me of the change in the Prince. I was sitting outside on a bench in the garden, thinking about the last time I was able to do this and he walked up and sat right next to me.

"You look different." He said.

I didn't know how to take that. *Different like I have spinach in my teeth? Different like I am getting as big as the Princess?*

"Different how?" I said, curiously.

"I don't know. Happy maybe." He said sarcastically.

"Ha-ha." I said and I punched him in the arm. That actually hurt my hand. Ow. He was really buff.

I thought about that and said as I looked down, "I don't know what to feel. I've actually had a pretty decent day. I was just thinking to myself how I haven't gotten to sit on a bench and enjoy the garden in a really long time."

He leaned back, putting his arms behind his head, "I know what you mean. I've had a pretty good day too. The Prince seems different." Then he stretched and yawned, putting his arm around me awkwardly. "It's a good different."

I sat up and starting to kick a rock and blush. *Was he putting his arm around me? Me the nerdy goofy girl? I thought he was into blondes? Listen to me, he finally makes a move and I am resisting him. I'm such a ditz.*

He leans down on his knees while sitting, and threw a rock in one of the long pools, nearly fourteen skips. *Wow, was he good at everything?*

I bent down to pick up a flower. I start to gather a bouquet, not knowing what to do with him sitting there actually talking to me. "M.P.... I mean....The Princess as well. Something is going on. I am actually suspicious on all these sudden changes of heart. I not really one to trust people."

He laughed and skipped another rock, which splashes a little water onto my shoes. *Great.* "You are too much. There's nothing to be suspicious about. I actually think that whole episode in the village the other day really humbled our bosses."

"I just don't think that they could really change that quickly." I remarked, picking a flower's petals.

"Well, keep your eyes peeled." He said, "I believe that people can have a change of heart, no matter how they started."

I could hear my call bell sound all the way out from the garden, I took my bouquet and ran up to see what I was needed about. I was hitting myself, knowing that I couldn't have said some other things while having a private conversation with the hottest man in the kingdom, like "Hey, I've liked you for ten years?" No too creepy or maybe "I'm hotter than I look?" No, too desperate. See I can't even flirt to my imaginary guy in my head. I'm hopeless.

Maybe at the ball I can keep my big mouth shut and just look pretty. But seriously, that might be hard to do when it doesn't usually come naturally to me.

-- -- -- -- -- --

Haggle and Smith got ready to go in the dark. They were both a little nervous about tonight. It was their big chance to prove that they could do anything. Their pipes steamed with smoke as they laced their old boots. After tonight exchange, they could soon buy a hundred pairs of brown leather shoes.

"Do you have the money from the boss?" Haggle asked Smith.

"Does it look like I'm stupid?" He answered while wiping his hands with a handkerchief.

"Did you get the men from the pub?" Said Smith to Haggle.

"Of course I did you nimrod. I know what our job is tonight."

They walked towards the pub, nodding to some big men smoking outside. They all walked together in silence up to the palace. *Clink, clink* went the money in the pockets of the big men. Their stomachs and wallets were full. They were ready to go.

They knew it was a perfect night for a crime because the palace was filled with people. Perfect crimes usually happen in the chaos of massive amounts of people, especially ones that were too occupied with the punch and the crabmeat then one missing person

-- -- -- -- -- --

Áron, Emmi and Kai were picked up in a royal carriage. This time their ride was smooth. The newly paved road was the highlight of the little town now. Workers had just finished their job that night in time for the many visitors coming to the palace.

Áron was wearing his black slacks and black polished riding boots. His cream shirt was simple and fitting. He did not look flashy like he knew the other royal patrons would be, but he was dressed the best that he could.

Emmi wore a simple green spring dress, one that she had been working on all week. Her sleeves three-quarter length were flattering on her small frame. The ribbon in her hair was small, but matched the fabric of her dress.

Kai of course wanted to be as noticeable as possible, but lacking the funds or the means, choose to have

Emmi make her a simple pink dress with lace on the bottom. How Kai dreamed of walking into the palace with a gaudy feathered hat with sparkles and diamonds. But she would have to pretend for now.

They *clip-clopped* up past the town and past their little farm to the royal streets. They could hear the music of the orchestra warming up from the castle's grand ballroom. They could smell the scents of tilapia, crab, lobster, veal and mutton. Scents they have only wished to experience with their own taste buds.

Banners and trumpeting servants greeted other royal guests at the gate. The castle was lit with colored lights, making it look like a far away place. It was going to be a magical night.

6: THE MUSIC IS CALLING

Emmi was breathless as she entered the castle gate. There were balloons, streamers, and children dancing around. There were musicians strumming and faces smiling. Everyone gazed at them, but accepted them quickly into the party culture.

As they entered the front entrance of the castle, she saw the Prince, the Princess, Priscilla and the dark-haired young man. She blushed and looked down at her simple dress. She felt plain amidst all the beautiful gowns, makeup and shoes.

She looked over to Kai. She was waving as a princess would. She was totally oblivious to Emmi's feelings or her plain dress, she was having the time of her life. And for that, Emmi smiled knowing that for the sake of her sister, she needed to enjoy the evening.

Áron saw Priscilla, in a blue gown, simple and yet elegant. She had little blue shoes on. Her hair was pulled to the side and curls bounced as she walked toward him. Her diamond drop earrings pulled the attention toward her pretty face. She was pretty in a simple way. Not over done, like the Princess, who was obviously trying hard to be elegant.

Priscilla had warm honey eyes that danced here and there with expression as she talked. Áron got lost in the movement. Her lips smiled often with laughter. Priscilla could tell that Áron was looking at her. She blushed and looked down.

Immediately, Priscilla knew that Áron was a gentlemen. She was caught away by his manner as he helped his younger sister down the carriage. Roderick was already helping Emmi down with a strong hand.

Roderick held his hand out to Emmi and bowed and kissed her hand.

He looked up at her and said in a debutant tone, "I don't believe that we have been introduced, m' lady."

Emmi turned away with a shy shoulder. She definitely wasn't used to acting like royalty. But she decided to play along. "We have not, my name is Emily Anne Sika. But everyone knows me by Emmi."

Roderick wrapped her hand around his arm, "My name is Roderick Braun. You cannot know my middle name until we have been better acquainted."

Emmi laughed, "Well, hopefully this evening, we can fix that problem."

Roderick smiled with anticipation.

The Sika family was escorted into the grand hall where the dancing and the music had begun. Then they went into the large dining room to have hors d'oeuvres.

Even the starter dishes were extravagant. There were Clams Casino with Pancetta, Dried scallops and beech nuts, and Caviar with Potatoes and Crème Fraiche.

-- -- -- -- -- --

I was too nervous to really eat the gorgeous appetizers. I am always awkward in formal social situations. You would think that a lady in waiting would be the most knowledgeable to all the right customs and the how-tos of royal dinner parties. But to be honest, I was only just used to getting a toothpick here, getting another napkin there, adding another log to the fire, bending down to the ground to pick up M.P.'s earring that had nearly fallen in her soup.

Let's just say that at the palace school, I tried hard to be the most elegant and graceful lady in manners class, but my natural clumsiness always took precedence. My tutor would always say that I was "Little Miss Hopeless Girl." Talk about a great uplifting knickname, that would be written down as an epic memorable name for legends to come. I could see it now, *The Adventure of the Little Miss Hopeless Awkward Girl and Her Dashing Prince.* Oh yes, definitely a best seller.

I snap back to reality. The Prince and the Princess were having fourths on the hors d'oeuvres. Which I thought was funny because they were hors d'oeuvres. I mean that's the point right, just to whet your appetite for the real dinner. But I knew to them, every meal was to be fully enjoyed.

Roderick looked at them and gave me a big, fat fish face right at me. I couldn't hold my laughter in any more. I am kind of glad that I did laugh though, because it totally broke the silence. Áron looked at me as if to say, "What so funny?" I looked at him, looked at Roderick cracking up, looking at Emmi looking all nervous, looked at Kai dancing around in her own world, looked at the royals so involved in the food and I finally decided something, that we were all funny in our own little ways. And then everyone started laughing. Big hallway-filling laughs.

I saw the Princess wipe her bass sized mouth with the corner of a dainty napkin. She announced in a loud voice that she was taking the two girls to her personal dressing room to get ready for the ball.

That was my cue to move. I knew that this was going to happen. All day I was in charge of organizing this little interlude. And for once, it was a job that I kind of enjoyed.

I saw the Prince put his arm around Áron and nod to do the same. They left the table to go to the Prince's chambers.

I saw Kai's face, completely in a trance of happiness. Emmi looked a little suspicious of the Princess' offer. I was shocked myself at first when the Princess told me her plans. I remember thinking, *that is really nice of her, but are these little skinny girls going to fit in any of her dresses the size of tents?* But when I saw the finished products for the girls, I knew that they were going to be very excited. Heck, I was excited, and it wasn't even my big night.

Upstairs in the Princess' wing there was at least ten tailors, seamstresses, hair designers and makeup artists. Some sample gowns were already on display on mannequins. There were elegant, sparkly gowns with pink feathers and there were simple, classy gowns with small lace.

I could tell Kai was totally eyeing the feathered dress. Emmi was looking bashfully at the simple gowns. I honestly felt happy for them and a little sad for myself. *How come the Princess took all these long years to be nice? Totally not fair. I was living with her for ten years and not once did she let me wear fancy jewelry and beautiful hand-made gowns.*

But I knew that the second that I thought these thoughts, I dismissed them. This is no time to be emotional. I knew I shouldn't complain, but I should just enjoy the night and make it a memorable evening for this family, because for them, this was a dream come true.

-- -- -- -- -- --

Áron walked up the long staircase to the Prince's wing. He didn't really know where to go. He had never been in the palace, much less the private suite of the Prince. The Princes and Roderick kept having to direct him this way and that.

Áron entered the wing. He was astonished at the sight. It was the most beautiful room that he had ever imagined. Gold lamp stands and red and gold curtains dangling from large ten foot windows. Even the wool carpet was lined with gold tassels.

When they entered, three tailors were there finishing up a few suits on mannequins. One option, Aron knew right off the bat was too much, blue jacket with about a hundred medals on the pocket and a frilly collar. The boots he likes though, sturdy, strong and black. Unlike his scuffed up work boots.

The second outfit's pants were alright, a dark grey, but the shirt was all wrong- bright red with a huge necklace. Áron laughed to himself imagining him walking down to dance with Priscilla in a chucky heavy breastplate of rubies. Way too much.

The third outfit had a long black coat that flared down to the back of his legs. It was royal blue and the shirt was a simple white. The pants made him laugh, green with stripes. And the shoes were little blue heels with a gold buckle.

Áron was suddenly humbled at the Prince's request to get him dressed in a nice suit. He knew that his simple shirt and tie weren't fancy. But secretly he liked his simple attire. He wanted to look nice, but not like a peacock like the Prince. But he knew that he had to be thankful for the new clothes.

The Prince gestured to Áron and then waved an arm to the outfits. "Pick one and my men with fit it perfectly to you."

Áron didn't want to seem ungrateful. These were very expensive clothes that he had never seen anything like in his whole life. He knew he was a simple farmer and knew nothing of the latest fashion and culture. But he knew that he couldn't go down to see his family dressed up like a peacock.

Roderick could see his hesitation and spoke up, "Your majesty. Áron is a farmer. He might feel uncomfortable in these lavish outfits. Maybe we get to have him tell us what he wants."

Áron looked at him relieved that he didn't have to say what was on his mind. He looked at the tailors and said, "I would probably feel more comfortable in something simple."

The tailors nodded and discussed and measured him. They put the long blue coat on him with the white shirt. They tailored the grey pants to his long legs and found just the right size boots for his feet. Áron was so grateful that they had chosen each of his favorite pieces of the three outfits. Now he felt more like himself but regal at the same time.

Áron loved his new outfit. He looked in the mirror. It made him look tall and handsome. He was missing something though. He eyed Roderick's sword on his belt. Roderick pulled it out, admiring the handiwork. A sword would definitely be cool. Roderick motioned to a guard to get Áron one.

He could only imagine what outfits the girls were trying on right now and if they had the same reaction as him. He laughed seeing in his mind's eye Kai's expressions of happiness and elation at the beautiful royal gowns that the Princess would have for them.

-- -- -- -- -- --

I looked at the clock on the wall. It had nearly been two hours since they came up to the Princess' suite. Two hours. That would mean that M.P. and the Prince were probably getting hungry right now. They got hungry every two hours. Well, come to think of it, as did I, but it was because I was constantly running around and burning off calories. I didn't know what excuse the Princess and the Prince had.

I looked at the girls getting their makeup and hair done. They looked beautiful, both of them. It was so magical seeing their transformation from farm girls to fabulous.

I looked at myself in the mirror. I had gotten ready nearly five hours ago. And I looked it. After I got dressed this afternoon, I had helped the ladies in the kitchen and then helped get M.P., I mean "The Princess," into her dress. That was an hour process by itself. Now, after appetizers and helping the two Sika sisters, my hair was a little frazzled and my makeup was a little dim. I usually wouldn't care, but I knew that if I wanted to be confident, I had to look my best tonight. Especially tonight.

I was putting on some mascara when I heard the clock strike eight. It was time to go and eat dinner now. I turned around. The girl's faces were glowing. Especially sweet Kai. Kai's pink feather dress was perfect for her. Fun, frilly and she worked it for all it was worth. She twirled around, letting feathers fall to the ground. I wanted to stoop down and pick them up out of habit, but I stopped myself. Today I was just a guest. Not a lady in waiting. I could enjoy myself.

Emmi's beautiful soft pink gown was perfect for her blonde hair. The dress looked as elegant and classy as her. Small pearl drop earrings adorned her ears. Her gloves were cream. She looked like a beautiful swan.

The Princess of course looked as peacockish as ever. Feather and sparkles everywhere. Usually I would be annoyed at her wardrobe knowing that I would have to get her in and out of it to even let her go to the bathroom. But tonight, I didn't mind. I didn't mind at all. And for that reason it was going to be a great night.

-- -- -- -- -- --

Áron, Roderick and the Prince walked briskly down the stairs to where they were going to meet the ladies for dinner. Two hours had passed and both Áron and Roderick were getting excited about seeing their sweethearts.

They were not disappointed. Áron's breath was taken away yet again to see Priscilla's beautiful brown eyes shaded with light pink and silver, just enough to be mysterious. Roderick's heart fluttered when he saw Emmi. She was a beautiful rose that had blossomed in the night. Emmi blushed and turned her head to the side to hide her face.

Roderick came close and whispered to her ear, "Don't hide your face. You're beautiful."

Emmi blushed even more. It was rare that such a refined gentlemen paid her such a genuine compliment.

The Prince escorted his bride, who was of course as flirtatious and fun as ever. They both laughed, trying to outdo one another on compliments. It was actually the first time that Priscilla could remember them actually being nice to one another.

Roderick took Emmi's arm, Áron held out his hand for Priscilla and Kai looked cross. She slumped her shoulders a bit. There was no one to walk her down. A knight standing guard was secretly watching her and held out his arm to her. He slid off his mask to let her see his face, and she was glad that he did. His green eyes, the color of spring, were a beautiful compliment to her gorgeous pink dress.

He bowed, and his helmet clinked closed. He opened it again laughing, "My name is Timothy. I would be honored to escort you tonight." But then Timothy looked at Roderick, "Well, that's if it's okay with you sir."

Roderick laughed and waved at them, "Be my guest sir. Tonight is a party!"

Kai smiled, "Timothy. I like that name."

Timothy held out his arm to her, "And what shall I call my lady?"

Kai flushed, "Kai." Then she whispered in the knight's ear, "It's short for Kyla, but no one calls me that."

Then Timothy saluted and his helmet slammed shut again, "Yes ma'am."

Kai laughed, "You're funny. And by the way, I think it's okay to take off your helmet, unless of course you fear something falling on your head tonight."

Timothy took it off, his sandy brown hair was messy but soft. Kai straightened it out with a gloved hand. "There, I'm glad I can see your face now."

Timothy was smitten.

-- -- -- -- -- --

We all walked to the dinner table. Our dresses were shooshing and swishing. Kai's feather's were dropping,

Timothy was cha-chinging, Áron was squeezing my warm hand, Roderick was wiping his sweaty nervous brow, the Princess was clanging and the Prince was clopping. All in all, we were quite the over dressed and noisy crowd. But we were happy.

Dinner was a dream. Sparkling cider for Kai and Timothy, who was asked to join at the table. Light raspberry Champagne for us adults. Duck, veal, lobster tails, crab, caviar and exotic fruit dripped from center pieces laden with gold.

I had never eaten so much. And by so much, I had two whole plates. I regretted it though as soon as I felt my dress getting tighter. I wondered if the Prince and Princesses' outfit had built in expansion sections that when they ate and ate, their clothes grew bigger with them.

Everyone laid back in their chairs. I even caught Áron hiding a little burp. He didn't have to cover anything around here. Before the Princess got married, she could burp like a sailor and she didn't hide it. Ever since she got married, she was more timid and proper, but I knew that she had a big one coming. I was going to laugh hysterically if tonight was the night.

But the Prince broke the ice first. His burp was the biggest, loudest burp that I've ever heard. Roderick's was a close second, of course the Princess showed up Roderick's with a belch. But to all of our surprised faces came a fourth place burp from the timid Emmi.

Roderick even clapped. "Not bad he said."

Even the Prince nodded in approval, "I think she's a keeper."

I laughed when I saw Emmi's face. She was so embarrassed. She was horrified at her bad manners. It was like she didn't mean for it to come out, but it did. I didn't want her to be totally humiliated, so I burped a little, then Kai and Timothy followed. Then we all laughed until we were wiping our dainty eyes from crying so much.

-- -- -- -- -- --

That night after dinner, we all seemed like old friends. We acted as if we had known each other their entire lives. Roderick told stories of him playing pranks on his cooks as a young teenager. Even I joined in with some of my favorite castle memories.

"I remember the time when I was about twelve years old." I began. "I was sent to get some eggs from the market for the Princess' breakfast." The Princess looked curious to see what tale I was going to tell about her. I continued, "I got the eggs and then tripped up the castle stairs and broke them all over me right before getting to the kitchen. It was so embarrassing that I had to change my clothes. Then I had to run to the market again before it was too late."

The Princess fanned herself and said sarcastically, "Oh my, your boss seems pretty bossy to me for demanding such an inconvenient task." Then she hiccupped from one too many drinks.

I winked at her, "No, she's not that bad. She's quite nice actually." The Princess beamed. Even the Prince looked impressed, as if he just found out a new trait from his bride.

After a wonderful dessert, it was time to dance off all the rich food. Áron took my hand again and pushed out my chair. His hand was warm. He had the most beautiful blue eyes I've ever seen.

"Would you like to dance with me?" He said with a strong voice.

I put my napkin down on the table from my lap. "I would be honored."

He smiled at me.

I saw Roderick was doing his own moves to try to get Emmi's attention across the table. Emmi looked nervous and shy. But bold Roderick stood up and walked over to her side of the table and pushed out her chair, gesturing to the party. Then he offered his elbow at which she gladly took it. Even Timothy, offered to dance with her. He *clinged* and *clanged* as he walked.

I looked over to a servant at the door. She was always a good friend to me. Her name was Eliza. I said, "Eliza, would you mind escorting this young man to get changed for the ball?"

The knight blushed and bowed, "Thank you so much." Then I looked back and I saw him and Kai walking towards the staircase.

Áron squeezed my hand. I knew the music was calling us. I saw Roderick kiss Emmi's hand and lead her to the garden. I think the night was calling them. I looked over the tipsy rulers. I think more champagne was calling them.

We entered the grand ballroom. Lords, ladies, dukes, duchesses and other random people that I had never even seen before were all dancing. It was like a music box, everyone stepping and gliding so rhythmically.

I knew Áron didn't know any of the dances. I only knew a few steps of maybe one dance. I blushed, he blushed. But I could tell that he was getting his courage up.

He bowed and said, "Madam, would you like to dance?"

And just like that we waltzed in the middle of the floor. It was as if everyone just ignored us. They were just dancing around us and behind us. We were in our own world surrounded by the sounds of the orchestra and the dancing music box. I put my hand on his tall shoulder. His arms were tall and muscular, as if they had worked every day of his life. His face was tan, as if every day the sun kissed it. He leaned in closed to my face. Our noses brushed. I could feel me falling for his touch. He took my face in his hands, his lips were warm and salty as if every day I wanted to stay there and bask in the light.

7: SOMETHING TO BE DONE

Roderick would remember tonight for the rest of his life. Emmi was so strikingly beautiful, her blonde hair being kissed by the moonlight, the sound of the fountains and the frogs serenading them. He took in every minute: the way that she kept placing her fly away hairs behind her ears, revealing diamond earrings that whispered to him. She didn't say much, but he talked for the two of them. She just laughed and said "Fascinating," or "How exciting."

They meandered down the garden path toward the back gate. He knew that he wanted to kiss her. But he didn't want to be too pushy and draw her away.

He whispered close to her ear, "My middle name is Theodore. But if you tell anyone, I will never talk to you again."

Emmi laughed, "I promise not to." And she was very close now to his face, their noses touched. Then she drew away shyly. She had just met this man. She wasn't sure about him yet.

Awkwardly, they sat on a stone bench and her hands slid down his arm to take his hands. Then there were fireworks.

Literally fireworks. They sat on the bench in awe of the splendor of the booms and lights flashing. Her hand was squeezed against his in wonderment and anticipation. And then all of a sudden her body jolted and her hand let go to grasp her throat. Roderick, now in attack mode, drew his sword. He saw what was going on; there was a blade to her throat.

-- -- -- -- -- --

Prince Gabriel poured another glass of champagne for his bride. Isabella was definitely enjoying the evening. She was so joyful, full of life and she was actually quite funny. Gabriel loved the way that she went off into voices of characters that were in her stories. He was beginning to like the way that her singing pierced his ears, but tickled his heart. He liked himself this way too, just enjoying his new kingdom, enjoying his bride and enjoying his life.

They walked hand to hand laughing about an inside joke and complimenting each other on the beautiful evening, their attire and the food. They were both happy now and he wished that it would never end. He wished that he didn't have to be the responsible one all the time. What would the Council say to his attitude now? They were counting on him to fix the kingdom.

He pushed the thoughts away, tonight he was just Gabe. Not "The Prince," but just Gabe. Just him and Isabella now, hand in hand, like they had known each other for years.

They leaned up against the back gate and their faces were so close to one another that he could see the sparkles of her eye makeup that made her eyes magical and mysterious. Their lips brushed and then fireworks. Literally. They both turned away from each other to bask in the glow and the pomp of the glorious sounds and lights.

Then they both froze, their necks were suddenly cold with blades of steel against them. They both felt blows to the face. They were trapped. Large hands pushed them from the gate. Other large hands bound their eyes and mouth with fabric. Then Gabe and Isabella were thrown into a carriage of some kind. Then there was blackness.

-- -- -- -- -- --

Haggle and Smith motioned to their men, about ten in all and as beefy and they could imagine. Haggle put his pipe in his pocket. It was his special good-luck pipe. The pipe that had been with him through all his major jobs.

Tonight was the biggest job of all: kidnapping the Princess. By doing so, ransom would be paid, or a potential war would be started. In other words, chaos would ensue. Their plan was to get their nightly scraps from their nephew. While he would be there, they would have men pin him down to steal the keys and while everyone was dancing, somehow take the Princess.

Their plan did have a lot of holes it in, they knew it. They weren't masterminds when it came to this kind of thing. They usually just went with the flow and hoped for the best. Tonight though, they knew that they just couldn't wait for something to happen, they would have to act as soon as they saw an opportunity.

It was just their luck that the beautiful Princess was walking toward the back gate holding her prince's hand. It was almost pitch black, but she could make out a beautiful pink dress. The Princess was a lot skinnier here than the stories that they heard about her. They thought according to the stories she was a big fat pig that dressed like a peacock.

They didn't really have time to think tonight, they just had to do the job and get out of there. Haggle smoked his pipe and stroked his beard, Where *was their nephew? Oh well, they would have to try without him. The boss didn't say anything about not taking the Prince and the Princess. In fact, he would probably be proud of them for getting both instead of just one.*

Haggle then was so surprised and dropped his pipe when the saw the fireworks. Literally. There were fireworks. He covered his ears and motioned to his men to put a blade at the Princess's throat. The Prince tried to attack, but he was knocked unconscious and bound through the gate before he could do anything.

Then Smith pointed to the Prince's face that was previously hidden by the night. It was their nephew! With the Princess no less! Haggle thought, *What a scoundrel! Bravo nephew! Good thinking.*

Smith motioned to two large figures standing up against the fence about ten feet down next to a large shrub. Smith ran to check it out. His eyes widened. Their royal crowns were unmistakable. *They had captured the wrong people!* Smith motioned to his men to get the Prince and the Princess before the fireworks died down and all the guards went back on duty.

In a matter of minutes, their nephew's keys were found to unlock the gate. All parties, that were being captured, were knocked out and tied up. Finally, they had pushed everyone into their large black laundry carriage without alerting the castle guards. It was a pretty successful evening for them, they had done it. Well, they had sort of done it. They did have some loose ends to tie up, but for now, they got the Princess.

As soon as they pulled away from the castle, the fireworks stopped and they could hear cheering and clapping by all the villagers and the people at the party. Smith was driving casually, but not too casually. Haggle was elated, they had done it. It was like the dice had fallen in their favor.

Smith saluted to their men as he galloped away and the men took out their gold, time to hit the pub.

Haggle took off his cap and wiped his brow, time to relax, time for a smoke. He reached in his pocket for his lucky pipe and it wasn't there. His lucky pipe. *Well, lucky pipe, you definitely had a good run tonight.* But then he said a little prayer and hoped that it dropped into a bush or a shrub. If someone found it and traced it back to them, he didn't know what the boss was going to do with them. And he definitely hoped for Smith's sake that it didn't bite them in the butt.

-- -- -- -- -- --

I saw the fireworks from the back window. Áron was holding my hand and I was leaning on his shoulder. It was a magical evening. But it was getting late. And where were the royals, Roderick and Emmi?

I looked around the room. Kai and Timothy were perfect together. Both awkward, goofy, but having the time of their life. They were dancing and twirling around, Kai's feathers showering the ballroom with color. Timothy was now wearing simple black pants and boots. His white shirt and grey jacket complimented Kai's hot pink dress. His sword swayed and bumped as he twirled Kai around.

I looked around for Roderick in the party. No sign of the Prince either. And where the Prince was, Roderick was not far behind. Usually a stone's throw.

I asked Áron, "Have you seen your sister?"

He looked around, "No, not since I saw her leave with Roderick to the garden."

I looked around while biting my lip, "Well, maybe we'll walk down to the garden to spy on them."

Áron laughed, "Okay, but Emmi would kill me if she knew that we were checking up on her."

We got down to the garden. The night was still. The guards were standing guard. Nothing was out of the ordinary.

"Have you seen Roderick?" I asked one of them.

The guard shook his head, his armor clanked,"No ma'am. During the fireworks, everyone was preoccupied.

But before that he was around here." Another guard poked him in the ribs. They whispered and jabbed, "Maybe you should check around some bushes for some smooching." They both laughed.

Áron rolled his eyes, a little annoyed that his sister would be quickly "smooched" after only knowing Roderick for a short time.

They heard a *clip-clop* of a servant coming down the garden path.

"Priscilla! I am so glad I found you." Could you help me look for the Prince and Princess?" I was about to serve second dessert, but I needed them to taste which one they would like first.

The Princess and the Prince missing out on second dessert? Something was very odd indeed.

"I am sorry," I say. "I haven't seen them recently. I was upstairs in the ballroom while I thought the Princess and the Prince went walking around the terrace."

The servant bowed her head and walked back up.

"I am getting a little concerned right now," I say.

Áron squeezed my hand. He was getting worried as well. I could see it in his eyes. He didn't have to say anything to let me know that his sister was on his mind.

8: TRYING TO BE FOUND

Emmi went in and out of consciousness. She was in some kind of dark carriage. Her hands are tied together. Her head was leaning against Roderick's shoulder. She heard snoring from the seats across from her. It was so dark. A little window from the back exit casted a little light off of something sparkly. The sparkles went in and out and around the room.

Emmi woke up again, this time Roderick had his strong arms around her. He was awake, but he was not speaking. His hands were tied and she was laying in his chest, feeling it rise up and down.

Her head ached and she tried to comfort it but her hands were tied too. She looked down at them and tried to scream, but her mouth was dampened by the nasty taste of a piece of rag. She was awake now and she was desperately trying to be free. Roderick's arm holds her down. He too is muzzled.

He motions to her to help him get his rag out of his mouth. He takes her rag out. It tastes like tobacco and is as black as soot.

"What is happening?"Emmi whispers to Roderick.

"I am not sure." Roderick looks around the carriage. *How long had they been out? Why were the Prince and the Princess here too? Where were they going?*

Both Roderick and Emmi were jumbled up with questions. Roderick heard some men talking up front and in a split second he knew who they were. They were his uncles.

He knew that if he yelled at them, he would give himself away as well. But the truth would eventually come. But now, he couldn't muster up the courage.

"Emmi," Roderick whispered. "We have to get our hands free." He motioned toward a crack in the bench, a perfect wedge to cut their hands free.

She cut her's first and guided his to be cut. Too bad he didn't have his sword now. Too bad he didn't have his work boots; he always had an extra knife in those. His uncles were smarter than he thought. What a perfect day to do a crime, the day that everyone was off guard.

Emmi heard the men talking again and whispered, "What do you they think their plan is?"

"I'm not sure, but I think I know what they are going to do with the Prince and Princess."

"What?"

"Hide them and wait for a nice ransom," Roderick answered.

"Well, what do we have to do with it?" Emmi said.

Roderick scratched his five o' clock shadow, "I don't know. But if we aren't the target that they have been after, then we have no use for us."

Emmi shuddered, "Meaning, if we aren't going to get them the money that they want than we are meaningless."

"Exactly."

Emmi saw the Prince and the Princess snoring happily. She started ripping a little of her beautiful pale pink dress and started slipping it ever so slightly out of the small caged window.

"What are you doing? said Roderick.

"Trying to be found." Said Emmi.

-- -- -- -- -- --

None of us had a good sleep that night. Poor Áron and Kai. This was supposed to be a wonderful and unforgettable evening for them. Áron was supposed to be pampered and have a royal bath. But instead of his warm bath, he stayed up all night scouring the castle grounds and asking everyone at the ball that night if they had seen his sister.

Kai was an emotional mess: crying on Timothy's shoulder, Aron's shoulder, my shoulder, and the cellar cat's shoulder. I honestly didn't know that you could physically cry that much. But surprisingly, you physically could.

I was up all night too. Not only were Roderick and Emmi missing, but the Prince and the Princess were too. Every servant was interviewed and every guard was interrogated by the Council. But it was a royal secret. No one could tell anyone outside of the palace. The Council was very specific about that. No one in the kingdom was allowed to know that their precious Prince and Princess were missing.

And lucky me, the Council had given me the responsibility to find them, me, a lady in waiting to the Princess, born of humble origins. They had given me the responsibility. Why? I have no idea. I mean I can guess. Maybe it's because I know the Princess best. Maybe it's because I am young and with me there is nothing to lose if I get hurt, injured or... gulp.

A hundred soldiers would probably be too conspicuous. A bunch of guards would probably too obvious. But a simple young lady, that was once a commoner, she would be able to blend in, ask questions, and go to and from and not be noticed.

Of course it had to be me. I didn't ask for this job in the first place. *Thanks dad for getting me into yet another appealing job.* I laughed to myself. If my dad was still alive, he would be proud of me though.

However, I was frightened and unsure. They left the hands of the kingdom to me, a young girl. I definitely needed to do a good job. Because if I didn't succeed, I would not only be unemployed but probably not be alive in order to live my dream. And I couldn't wait to live that dream of settling down and living a simple life again. What pressure.

Áron insisted that he come with me. Not only to protect me, but also to find his sister. I felt bad for him and would definitely need his help. Especially since we didn't know anything about these men or how many of them were out there. I know that I couldn't take down a few criminal masterminds myself.

I mean it would be quite funny to just roll up to their secret lair and announce, "Hello everyone, I'm just here to get the Prince, Princess, Roderick and Emmi back. So if you would be so kind." Yeah, that would be funny when they blow my head off with one shot.

Now, I am definitely in a pickle. I mean a real pickle. A big, crunchy, dill pickle. And I definitely need to find a way to get the job done, I and the whole kingdom are going to be reduced to a big, fat squished pickle. *Why am I talking about pickles? Maybe because I haven't had one of Mrs. Cuire's dill pickles in a while. Maybe I can get one before we go?*

-- -- -- -- -- --

That next morning Áron and I met to discuss our plan over a simple breakfast of pickles, toast and coffee.

"We should start from the very beginning and retrace all of their steps." He said.

I doubted we would find anything; the grounds and castle had already been scoured for evidence by every employed person of the castle. Believe me, I was in charge of looking in the dungeon and found nothing but rats and some old guys wanting some kisses from me. *Why do I always get assigned the dirty jobs? Do I have a sign on my face that reads, 'Need help doing something annoying and tedious? You've come to the right place.'*

I agreed with Áron and finished my coffee. I've never really liked the stuff, even growing up. But considering that this might be the last day of the rest of my life, I decided to give this stuff one last try. I took a warm sip, nope, still as disappointing as ever. I tried to recover my drink with two cups of milk and five cubes of sugar. That was a little better. Now I couldn't taste the coffee. I would much rather have hot chocolate. Now hot chocolate with whipped cream, that's a real woman's drink.

We gathered some supplies in knapsacks: some blankets, a pencil and some paper, some money and some food. We didn't know how long we would be gone. Then Áron kissed Kai on the forehead, telling her that she would be safer with Mrs. Cuire and her body guard Timothy, who was of course happy to be of assistance. We then waved to the cooks and servants that were waiting for us and then we left.

We started in the terrace where I had first seen The Princess and the Prince drink and drink some more. I sketched what everyone was wearing that night and any jewelry that I remembered seeing them put on. Any small piece of jewelry or a button might be helpful to solve the mystery. That's if we could find anything.

I read the report from The Council and wrote down any important details that I found. There weren't very many. The crime apparently happened while the fireworks were going off and everyone was distracted.

You would think that with this kingdom's security policies that a small five minute fire work display wouldn't be an issue. I mean I can't even go to the bathroom without getting a royal hall pass so to speak. "Where are you going ma'am?" Then I have to explain myself that I drank a little too much apple juice at breakfast time and that nature was calling.

So far, according to all the reports, the Prince and the Princess, Roderick and Emmi were both last seen in the garden near the back gate.

I drew a map of the castle and the grounds in my notebook and I circled the back garden. There had to be a clue somewhere there. I just knew it.

Áron was brooding with thoughts. I know I could see his brow furrow. He checked my notes and said, "So they were taken at the same place. Who has keys to that gate?"

"Very few people. Only the head chef, to go in and out to make deliveries, the head of the Council and the..."

Áron completed my sentence, "The captain of the guard. Isn't it?"

He saw my face turn white. "Do you think Roderick was in on this the whole time?"

I didn't want to blame Roderick. I knew that he was rough around the edges, but I've never seen him to any unethical or wrong. He was definitely loyal to the Prince and when he made a promise, he stuck to it.

But I couldn't get that one image out of my mind, the image of the night that I saw him sneaking food to the poor men outside this very gate. At least I thought it was food. Maybe I have been blinded the whole time and it was the crown's jewels, royal secrets or other contraband. What if Roderick was in on it the whole time?

I couldn't be sure. I didn't want to speak too quickly about what I knew. I didn't want to make the situation more complicated considering that Roderick had Emmi somewhere in this kingdom.

Áron saw me get lost in my thoughts, "Priscilla, you aren't telling me something about Roderick." He saw my head drop, "I know you are hiding something."

I told him, "I don't know what to think. I've always trusted Roderick and he has never let me down. Believe me, I would have told you from the beginning if I didn't trust him. But I can't forget about one thing."

“What is that?” Áron’s voice was shaking.

“An image,” I hesitated, “A memory.” Then I told him about that rainy and cold night.

After a moment of silence, Áron said, “You never said anything to him about this?”

“No, never. I didn’t want to expose him. I honestly thought it was a harmless thing, giving food to beggars.” My voice trailed off. “I guess I should have said something while I had the chance. Because now look where we are.”

-- -- -- -- -- --

“I couldn’t have planned it better myself.” A dark voice whispered to himself in the room. “The Royals are missing and now I have drawn away any rats that could spoil my plan.”

After a moment of silence, the voice continued, “Now, it is our time to move.”

-- -- -- -- -- --

Isabella woke up to a pounding headache. She definitely needed to not drink as much champagne last night. It was all a blur. She was laughing with Gabriel and enjoying a beautiful evening and then she was dreaming.

She remembered dreaming about being taken and being bound.

Isabella opened her eyes; it was so dark in the room that it must have been her bed. She loved it when it was dark as a cave. She never could get any sleep if there was even a peep of light shining. She would always ring the bell to have Priscilla close the curtain or give her an eye cover.

Isabella turned in her thoughts, the bed was much harder than before and there was a terrible smell in the room. It smelled like garbage, complete garbage. Isabella stirred awake and sat up, this was definitely not her room.

9: SAD NEWS

Haggle and Smith had a full day. They woke up late that morning, scratching their beards and drinking from dirty mugs.

They were both unsure of what to do. Haggle spoke up first, "Do you think that we need to tell the boss that we got the Prince and two extra people?"

Smith yawned, "That's a great idea Haggle. Why don't you just write to the boss, 'Dear Boss, we were such imbeciles that we couldn't even get the right Princess, so we got the captain of the guard, random courtier and the Prince. Hope you like them. Love, Haggle and Smith.'"

Haggle smoked a cigarette, "Well it's not my fault that I had never seen the Princess. It's not like we're in the castle all the time!"

Smith said, "I think we should just get rid of Roderick and his girlfriend. That way, there was no extra people to deal with."

Haggle looked at his brother, "You mean by getting rid of them, you mean forever?"

Smith shouldered his brother, "That's exactly what I mean."

"But Roderick is our nephew," Haggle whined.

Smith scratched his beard, "No loose ends. You know the boss' policy."

-- -- -- -- -- --

Emmi didn't know what to do. She and Roderick didn't sleep a wink in their seemingly abandoned warehouse. When they were dragged in the night before, they were fully conscience, but made their kidnappers believe that they were as unconscious as their hungover counterparts. They both knew that causing a disturbance first thing was probably not the best idea.

She could see the Princess and the Prince were stirring and waking. She knew that it was going to be so difficult to explain that "By the way, your highnesses, we were all kidnapped yesterday. But don't worry, Roderick and I have everything under control."

She could hear footsteps of the men outside. There seemed to be only two of them. Not like last night, where there seemed like a hundred men. Could she and Roderick take them out? They had no weapons, only Roderick's strength. But she didn't know what weapons the men had. The Prince and the Princess could be in danger as well if they skirmish. It was best not to make any sudden moves.

The two men open the large barn-like door.

One old man spoke, "Wakey wakey! Hope everyone slept well last night in our fine accommodations."

The Princess sat up and screamed as a rat skittled passed her. The other man jabbed his partner and laughed deep and hollow.

The Prince yoke up and yelled out, "What do you want with us?"

The old men threw in a bucket of slop. "It doesn't matter what we want with you. It just matters to the boss. And personally I am picking up that the boss just wanted you all out of the way."

Roderick yelled, "'Out of the way? What do you mean?"

Then the barn door slammed shut.

-- -- -- -- -- --

I was looking around the back gate for anything, any clue. It literally looked as if this place had been swept and clean. I could see little strokes of a broom. *You would think that since we were in charge of the investigation, that all evidence would remain untouched until we got there.* I thought to myself as I scuffed the floor with my shoe.

Maybe I needed another approach. I turned to Áron, "Maybe we look in the bushes and the plants. It's obvious that we won't find anything out in the open."

"Good idea," he said as he bent on his hands and knees to move over a leaf of a bush.

We had scoured the entire garden. We did find a few sparkles from the Princess's gown and even a pearl earring. I wrote all findings in my notebook, careful to draw each detail.

When Áron saw the pearl earring in my hand, I could see his mouth pout in sadness. It was Emmi's earring. We both knew it. Now I knew he was determined as ever to find her, dead or alive, but hopefully alive.

We got all the way over to the gate, where the crime had apparently happened. We searched bush after bush, thorn after thorn, shrub after shrub until we found something that I knew that we were meant to find: a wooden pipe.

Áron found it first. He held it up for me, "Did Roderick ever smoke?"

"No, never. No staff was allowed to smoke at the palace. The Princess has asthma." And then I looked at the wooden pipe in his hand. It looked worn and well-loved, but obviously handmade. The letter "H" was carved on it.

I sketched the pipe in my notebook and drew the tiny letter. *H. What an odd letter.* I honestly didn't know many people whose name started with "H," Well, I knew Harriet that worked in the kitchen and Hank that was the laundry man. Both worked in the palace so obviously it couldn't have been them.

"It's monogrammed!" Áron said as he looked at the pipe from all angles, "The workmanship is old, but good, like it was custom made. You would really have to find a master to know how to carve something like this. Since no one in the palace was allowed to smoke, the only assumption that we can make is that it belonged to someone that was in cahoots with the criminals."

"Nice alliteration," I said. I always had a bit of whit to break up an intense situation.

Áron looked up as if he was thinking, "Oh I can do better." Then he looked as if he had an idea, "Peculiar piped penned with plethora of puzzling problems."

"Ohh," I said clapping with approval, "Well done."

I sure hope he was right. Because right now, that was the only evidence that we had to hang the entire kingdom's fate on.

-- -- -- -- -- --

Haggle and Smith got a post that day. It was a letter from a "bakery" advertising their new cinnamon buns. But they knew who it was really from.

They opened it and a simple sentence was written very small underneath a picture of a warm delicious bun, "Get rid of the evidence."

Haggle looked at Smith and Smith looked at Haggle. They didn't sign up for this. Kidnap the Princess sure, make it look like pros did it, okay, but kill her and now the three others there, including their nephew? They better get paid their worth. This was by far the nastiest, guiltiest, most difficult thing that they ever had been asked to do. The blood of the innocent was going to rest on them. And they knew it.

They had their fill of guilt throughout their years of service. Haggle especially couldn't sleep a night without seeing her there, screaming and calling out for help amidst the flames. He could never forget that night for the rest of his life. It haunted him constantly, which was why he wasn't looking forward to adding a few more ghosts to his dreams.

Smith didn't speak of his dreams much with Haggle, probably to not appear weak, but Haggle knew the truth. They both were cursed men haunted by ghosts of their past.

Haggle especially wanted to get out of this line of work fast. He knew Smith had harder skin than him. Smith was kind of the brains of the operation, but Haggle knew deep down, he was a big softee.

They thought the original plan was to kidnap the Princess for a while, make the kingdom go in upheaval, start a war or something, then after some time, when they got paid off and living the high life, the Princess would return and every one would rejoice. At least that is what the boss said that he would do.

But now that the Prince was gone as well, had the boss changed his plans out of desperation? Haggle knew that something had to be done. Maybe before anything went down today, he would free everyone and make it look like they got away. But then he would be a wanted man. What had he gotten himself into? It started with some innocent jobs, stealing chickens, burning down buildings, but not this, not murder. And definitely not killing family.

They decided that gassing them would be the most humane. They prepared the bottles while wearing masks, and made their way over to the warehouse. But when they got there and opened the door, death's smell was already creeping out of it.

Smith peeked in and saw that everyone was covered in blood and laying very still. Their nephew especially looked as if he had tried to fight, but lost brutally. Smith crossed himself for the sake of his nephew, hoping that his soul would be at peace.

He let Haggle peek inside. It was true. They both hung their hats in a moment of silence. Haggle wiped a small tear from his face. Smith closed the warehouse door and nudged Haggle toward the carriage.

The deed had already been done. But by who? They had no idea. Maybe the word got out about the kidnapping and the reward and other scum like them beat them to it. Maybe the boss hired other people to do the dirty work, knowing that Haggle and Smith would have second thoughts.

They didn't want to find out. They were just glad that it was all over and they could collect their money. The boss should be happy with them. They did everything that he asked of them and more. They even had to nerve to ask for a little extra for getting the Prince and the two other people.

They gathered their things, loaded up the carriage and headed to make a delivery to the castle. They found some chickens to steal from a local farmer and threw them in their carriage. They couldn't show up empty handed and just ask to come in. They were smarter than that and they knew it.

-- -- -- -- -- --

"Are they gone?" whispered Emmi to Roderick. Roderick quietly motioned for everyone to stay down and he looked through a small gap in the wall.

“They left.” He said. “But I still want to stay here for a few minutes to see if anyone else is coming.”

“Roderick, I trust you with my life, but this is the most disgusting thing that I have ever had to do.” Prince Gabriel whispered.

“I’m sorry Sire, but this is the only way that we could get free.” Roderick whispered back.

Then there was silence. No footsteps, no talking, no people. Roderick looked around to see if anyone was around and he slowly got up. He walked softly around the perimeter of the warehouse, checking every hole he could find. Being quiet was very difficult since there was hay strewn all over the ground.

After a few minutes he motioned for everyone to get up. The coast was clear!

-- -- -- -- -- --

I held the pipe in my left pocket as Áron and I left for the village. We had changed into worker’s clothes, so as not to cause any suspicion. It felt good to wear boots again and soft cotton dresses. I always grew tired of wearing itchy wool and large corsets. Wearing old clothes and boots made me feel that I was back living again in my old life.

I remembered my last encounter in this village. That was where I met Áron and his family. I would never forget that day. That‘s the day that his blue eyes captured me so deep that I knew that I wanted to get to know him better. That day was the day that I discovered how kind he and his family was, and how opposite the royals were. That's when I discovered that I wanted to leave my royal living forever.

I've never really wanted to leave the palace, knowing that this was what my father wanted from me. But, I knew that someday I would have to grow up and make my own path. That day was today. After doing this job for the sake of the kingdom, I was going to hang up my apron forever and live a simple life. Hopefully, Áron felt the same about my future.

The smell of the bakery down the path was overwhelming. I always liked the smell of waking up to fresh bread and croissants from the palace. I would always sneak in and grab a small piece of the smoking loaves between running an errand for M.P. *Do I actually miss that place? Wow, it almost sounded like I had a fond memory there for a second.*

My tummy gave a little rumble. It was only ten o'clock in the morning and I was already hungry. I knew this would happen. I usually have to eat every two hours or I get pretty cranky.

Áron could see that I was looking down at my belly. He laughed, "Hungry already? We've only just begun our journey."

He took my hand and led me to his farm very near the bakery. Of course he recruited me to feed the pigs and milk the poor cow. But I didn't mind. I rather be kicked from a cow then kicked in the face from the Princess when she was getting her corset on. I got two black eyes from that and believe me it stung for three days.

Then we went inside the cottage after our chores. Áron unwrapped a soft loaf of bread. It was rich and hearty, like pumpernickel. We had a little butter spread on top. It was a perfect snack to begin the day.

The soft bread reminded me of when my mother would bake. She never had the fanciest kitchen or the rarest ingredients like the castle, but her food was made with the great ingredient ever: love. And every time we ate together, the smells, the richness and the love made our dinner more inviting and special than any exotic meal that I had ever had at the palace.

Áron could tell that I was in my own thoughts. "What are you thinking about?"

I laughed, "I was just having a moment with this bread, it is so good."

"Thank you," He said smiling. "This is our family's deepest darkest secret, so if I tell you, I'll have to kill you."

I jabbed him, "Alright, I won't ask." I took another bite of the soft loaf and drank a little of the morning's cream. I continued, "But in all seriousness, it just brought back memories about my mom. She was a wonderful cook."

He put his bread down and looked deep into me, "If you don't mind me asking, how did she die?"

I looked down, "It was terrible. She was trapped in a fire and couldn't get out."

Áron gulped, "Your barn was set on fire?"

I looked at him with my head cocked to the side, "How did you know it was the barn?"

He hesitated, "I just figured as much. You said that your mom and dad were farmers and that they raised sheep.

You don't have very many buildings on a farm that raises sheep except a barn and a house really."

A moment passed then he reached for my hand, "I'm so sorry. That is terrible. But she must have been a wonderful woman."

I looked up and half-smiled, "She was."

Then there was a *thump, thump, thump.* Like someone was banging on a door. Áron and I got up to look out the window.

There was a man pounding a sign to a post across from the bakery. Some people gathered to see. Áron and I left the house to have a look.

By the time we got there, people were leaving the post crying and holding one another. I looked confused. What could be the news?

We read,

> The Prince and Princess have both died tragic deaths on the same day. Both kings also died of broken hearts after hearing the news. This week will be a week of mourning for the entire kingdom. The Council will resume its place to rule instead of the monarchy until a new monarchy is chosen according to the Law of Saint Beatrice.

We were both in shock. The Princess and the Prince were dead? The kings were also dead? I knew that both were in bad shape, but how could this be? How did anyone know that the Prince and the Princess were dead? What about Emmi and Roderick who were with them?

Something didn't seem right. The Council has sent us to find them and told us "Not to make it a big deal around the kingdom that the Prince and the Princess were missing because we didn't want to alarm anyone of their whereabouts." But now the whole kingdom knew.

I read the post again, "The Law of Saint Beatrice." *What was that one again? Gosh, how long had it been? It had only been two years ago that we had to study all the laws and the saints of the kingdom for the past five hundred years. Was I just sleeping in that class?*

I remember the law had something do with being valiant and the people. Something about if there is a situation where the Prince and the Princess didn't have an heir to rule, and then the people could choose someone brave to rule instead.

I remember this lesson because at the Regional Royal School, Roderick was a student with me. In fact we had been in class together since age ten. I remember one day during the lesson about Saint Beatrice, Roderick was flirting with some fellow attractive female classmate and when the professor talked about getting elected to be king, I remember Roderick held up his little slip of paper that said, "Vote for me!"

The class all had a good laugh then and the flirtatious blonde wrote down her address and slipped it to him. How come it was so easy for Roderick to get a date? Totally not fair. I had to go with Freddy Lancaster that year to the school dance, and believe me he wasn't anything to brag about. The whole dance, he went on and on about his mole on his face.

And yes I was a little jealous of Roderick then. And yes I kind of wanted to be that cute blonde that got all of his attention. But I am over Roderick now. I feel sorry for him now, not knowing where he was in this vast kingdom. What if he and poor Emmi were dead as well? I didn't even want to think about that possibility.

I snapped out of my dreams. Back to reality. I looked at Áron's face. He was mortified. I knew that he was determined now to finish the job. If not to find the missing royals, find out what happened to his sister. I felt sorry for him. I couldn't imagine being in his shoes: not knowing if he would find or bury his sister before this mission was done, no matter how much time it took.

10: THE WHITE ROOM

Roderick motioned for everyone to stand up. He hid a little laugh. Everyone looked like zombies, literally. Everyone's hair was a mess, makeup was smeared, clothes ripped, blood rubbed all over everyone's face and body.

It was Emmi's idea of killing a rat and smearing the blood on everyone's clothes, much to the chagrin of the royals who would never, ever think of doing such a disgusting thing. But there was just not enough time to explain, they just had to act quickly.

Roderick, especially, knew that their time was short. He could hear the men waking up and coming around the corner. He knew their voices. He knew that at any moment, they could expose him for what he was. He needed a plan that would save all of them at the same time so that no questions could be asked. He didn't want to explain that this whole ordeal was his fault, or his family's fault.

He was glad that Emmi thought of the idea to kill all of them off. She was quick on her feet, a characteristic that he would have never guessed about her. She always seemed so shy and guarded. But when it came to working under pressure, she was strong, brave and level-headed. He liked that very much. He could see that the Princess under pressure was a basket case.

The Princess looked down at her blood stained dress. She did a little gagging sound, "I think I'm going to be sick." She went to leave the barn.

"No!" the Prince whisper-shouted. "You'll be quite the sight if anyone sees you outside."

Tears came to the Princess' eyes, "What can we do? I need a bath, now!"

Roderick looked around through a hole in the warehouse. No one was around. He turned to everyone. "I am going to sneak around to see what needs to be done."

Roderick quietly slipped through the door to scout for a safe place. It was a pretty abandoned lot. He continued walking to a shack where his uncles had clearly been sleeping. A small dirty tub was in the corner.

Roderick's feet stepped on something hard and circular, then another small object. He looked down; it was too dark to see. He bent down and brushed away the grass. Two gold coins.

He walked outside to see his findings in better light. They were not only coins, they were royal coins. The type only found in the castle. Regular peasants like his uncles would not have access to them. All the village people used copper or nickel farthings. But gold coins, they were rare.

He went back to see if there was more. He rummaged through the floor and he found four more. Six coins. Definitely enough buy four cloaks and a small dinner for all of them, with one coin left keep as evidence.

Roderick put one coin in his pocket and held the others. He ran to the warehouse to tell the others where he was going. He showed them the direction of the dirty bathtub. His party looked inside the little room, much to the disgust of the Princess who would "Rather die than be in such a filthy place." Roderick laughed and said to the Prince, "She's all yours."

Then Roderick left them and exited the compound to find anyone that would sell him four cloaks.

-- -- -- -- -- --

The castle was in mourning. All the flags were half mast. The servants were glum and had tear-stained eyes. Mrs. Cuire was especially saddened by the news. Not only would she have to now have to answer to the Council members, but she would also have to be the local counselor. She had already turned her little kitchen into a room for any servant to come in and cry.

Kai and Timothy had visited every day to see how the others were doing. Kai had rolled up her sleeves and started helping around the castle. She was a hard worker and she enjoyed doing the things that most servants hated.

Mrs. Cuire admired Kai's spirit. Most young girls who's sister was missing and possibly dead, would be emotional. But not Kai. She was cheerful, optimistic and encouraging. Mrs. Cuire would always hear her say, "I don't know what's going on, but my brother will found out. He can fix anything." Mrs. Cuire knew that Kai was still young and acted immaturely sometimes. But ever since the grave news came over the castle, Kai seemed to blossom into a strong young lady.

Mrs. Cuire was suspicious. She thought that it was odd that on same day, the Prince, Princess and the two Kings die all at the same time. Also, Roderick and Emmi turn up missing on the same night. Someone was not telling the servants and staff the real story, Mrs. Cuire knew that for sure. But she had to be strong for the others. She also didn't want to get into trouble snooping around and letting little ears hear her doubts. She definitely wanted to keep her job for when something did happen to change all this, hopefully sooner than later. She said a little prayer for Priscilla and Áron to come to a conclusion about the great mystery quickly.

-- -- -- -- -- --

I didn't even know where to start looking. All I had was a little wooden pipe with some grimy initials in it. What a mess I was in. I couldn't believe that the Kings, Prince and the Princess were dead, Roderick and Emmi were missing and all we had was some wild goose chase from a little wooden pipe.

Áron looked as lost as me. "Well, maybe we start asking around town to see if anyone knows of a pipe carver in the area."

I nodded "Sounds logical."

Áron could tell that I was unhappy. He could see the look in my eyes. He put his arms around me, "Priscilla, I know it's really hard for us right now. We don't know where the Prince and the Princess are and Roderick and my sister are missing. We just have to have faith that the good guy is going to win."

I laughed, "Good guys only win in stories."

He squeezed my shoulder, "Well then, I guess we are in the middle of one now." He let go and nodded toward the Thatcher shop. "Let's get started before it gets too late."

-- -- -- -- -- --

One store after another we visited. No one wanted to say anything, or they had no idea what we were talking about. The butcher even laughed at us and said, "A pipe maker? Who does that crazy job? Real men put food on the table- literally." Then he impressed us by dropping a huge twenty-pound flank on the chopping block in front of us.

I looked discouraged. Áron reached for my hand and said "Thank you" to the butcher before leaving.

He pulled me toward the side alley. "Priscilla, maybe we are looking in the wrong places. We've been asking good and honest people to help us find a criminal or someone that worked with criminals. Maybe we have to ask criminals were to find criminals."

I laughed, "Have you seen you and me? We don't exactly look like a bunch of criminals."

"Well, maybe that's the problem." He laughed. He pulled me toward the road. "Here, let's go to my house. I have an idea."

-- -- -- -- -- --

Roderick walked into the local town. He had been walking for a little while, maybe twenty minutes. He wasn't familiar with this town, but then again, he hadn't really gotten out much. He could see the Castle in the distance. It looked sad and grey. The bright colored flags were not hoisted and the sky around it was cloudy and sad.

Roderick thought to himself, *I wonder if the kingdom knows what happened to us?*

His question was soon answered when he entered the town. People were all wearing dark colors and walking around heavy hearted. The usual loud market places were calm and everyone was slow and whispering to one another.

He saw a group of people paying respects to a sign posted on a wooden board. He read the sign. His heart ached with emptiness. Now he understood. The Prince and the Princess were claimed as dead. The two Kings died as well. He knew that the post was wrong about the Royals, but he wondered about the two Kings. They were good men. He had a moment of silence for them and lowered his head. Now he was determined to figure out was going on in the Kingdom.

He remembered the sign again, "The Law of Saint Beatrice." He smiled remembering his school days and that particular lesson. The Tutor was talking about a valiant man or woman being voted to take over the job of being the new ruler if there were no heirs to the throne. Roderick remembered holding up a sign to make the class laugh. That's all he was, the class clown then. But in all seriousness, he would never be voted King. He was a street rat turned body guard with a family tree that would shame any Royal. He knew that no matter how hard he tried, being voted to be King was a dream that would never come true.

Roderick had taken off his outer tunic and had on his white dirty undershirt. It was little cold out and windy. He needed to find a cloak before he started shivering. His usual pristine boots were muddy and straw covered. His black pants were just as dirty. His hands and face were scraggly and grubby. He looked around at the town. He fit right in.

He felt the coins in his hands. They were the only thing that was keeping him from exploding from the thought of hunger and insanity.

He passed booth after booth. Nothing of interest to him. All jewelry, fruit, wooden bowls and pots. But even these items couldn't compare with the beauty of the things inside the palace. Even the jewelry that the Royals and Emmi were wearing could be something that these people would love to steal and make a killing on. That reminded him, when he got back, he must tell everyone to take off all of their jewelry. Even their glittery shoes would bring unwanted attention to them.

Finally Roderick found a little booth connected to a home that had little wooden toys and hats for sale. He entered. He was so tall that he had to bend down to get through the door. Only an old lady was at a loom near the back. Roderick looked around the home. No one was in sight except an old woman at the loom. He was glad, he didn't want anyone in the background running and telling the others that he had royal coins. He could create quite a stir.

Roderick cleared his throat. The old lady looked up to him. She was surprised at his height, but his clothes gave her nothing to be alarmed at.

"Can I help you?" She said while looking down.

"I was wondering if you sold cloaks?"

"Do I look like a clothier?" She said annoyed. "Can you read? The sign says 'Toys N Hats.'"

Roderick had never heard someone so rude. "Well do you know where I can find anyone that sells cloaks?" He was fiddling with the coins in his hand now with such force that one little coin slipped out onto the floor.

The lady looked up. "I know that sound. That's not a village farthing. That's a deeper, richer sound." She looked frightened.

She got up hurriedly and closed her shop door. "I don't want any trouble young man. Not this time. Not with the Kings, the Prince and the Princess being gone and such. You can tell whoever you work for that my husband or I won't do any more secret carving jobs for him or his cronies. I'm a good honest woman. I have a family and grand-children. Any more gold coins and my husband will be suspicious." Then she pointed to the door and pushed Roderick out.

"Ma'am please listen to me, I'm am not with these criminals. I'm a servant of the Prince and I need your help."

She stopped pushing him and pulled him close. She studied him for a minute. "I believe you young man. You are much too handsome to be part of some band of old thugs." She eased her grip on his shirt, "Tell me more."

Roderick didn't know if he could trust this little lady. She could be part of the plot for all he knew. But he had to take a chance. The kingdom was counting on him. Emmi was counting on him.

"Ma'am, what if I told you that the Prince and the Princess are very much alive and are in need of some help?"

The lady looked at him suspiciously, "I would say that you are not telling the truth."

"What if I said that if you help me get the Royals, a servant of theirs and myself a cloak then I will tell of your good deeds to be rewarded at a later time?"

The lady looked even more suspicious. "Then I would say that you are up to something."

Roderick didn't know what to do to convince the old lady. All he had was the clothes on his back and his coins.

"I am going to tell you what happened to the Prince and the Princess, but I need you to believe me." He paused to look at the lady's face and it was calm and serious. He continued. "Last night during the celebration, my friend Emmi and I were at the ball and we were walking toward the back gate of the castle. We were taken and bound in a carriage. Then the Prince and the Princess were taken as well. Everyone was knocked out and taken to some warehouse twenty minutes from here. I heard that the evil men were going to kill us all, so my friend devised a plan for us to commit suicide of sorts and then hopefully the bad guys would run away. It worked. Now we are starving and naked and I alone here to get them food and clothes."

The women looked at Roderick so serious that he could see the wrinkles around her blue-green eyes.

She looked at him for a long time and finally asked, "Tell me young man, what color is the throne room?"

Roderick cocked his head, not knowing why this question was relevant, "Umm, it's white. All pure white."

The women smiled, "Now, young man, I believe you."

Roderick was unsure what to say.

The woman continued, "When I was a little girl, my father was a very talented hatter. This was many, many years ago. He was commissioned to make a special hat for the king himself during a special ball. I remember he took me with him. He had made three very special hats for the king. Ones with rare peacock feathers, rhinestones, diamond bits and sapphire. They were the most beautiful hats that I had ever seen. We were given money to pay for our expenses of course. My father lived off those gold coins his entire life."

The women looked far away into the window, "I still remember the day that we were escorted into the throne room. It was the prettiest site that I ever saw. The throne room was white. Pure white. Everything from the vases with white feathers, to the marbles columns, to the throne it's self. My father told me later that everything was pure white so that you would focus on the King on the throne. And aye, did we. He was the most gentile man that I ever had met."

The women turned toward Roderick, "Young man, only a servant of the crown would know what the inside of the throne room looked like."

Roderick showed her the coins, but she refused, "I would give the shirt off my back for that king's kin any day." She went inside the back door and came out with four large cloaks.

"Keep your money young man. In fact, here is a day's wage worth of farthings. You can buy a meal for all of you. I wouldn't want anyone to get suspicious about your ware-a-bouts. This town is full of little crooks that would take advantage of anyone that could give them a break. Those gold coins would give you away for sure."

Roderick was speechless. This old woman gave him a small felt sack with an entire day's wage. He bowed low before her, "Ma'am, your service to the crown will never be overlooked."

He looked into her wrinkled face. He could tell that in her glory days she was beautiful. She still was to someone. She had a good heart, he could tell. Even though she had once aided his uncles, he knew that she wasn't scum like them.

He put on the long brown cloak and tied the small sack on the inside string. He held the other three cloaks in his arm and left to find the other members of his party. He had been gone for over an hour; he didn't want them to worry.

11: Torn Pieces

Roderick returned to the warehouse. He only found the Prince, who was in his underpants and undershirt.

"Where is everybody else?" Roderick asked, while turning his head and throwing the Prince a cloak. That was definitely a sight that he didn't want to see again for his entire life.

"The Ladies are hiding out, waiting for you to return. We have all taken baths and hidden our old clothes away, but as you can imagine, the ladies are in their undergarments."

Roderick laughed imagining, the Princesss and Emmi hiding out in the bathhouse waiting for their cloaks, waiting for him to rescue them from humiliation. He could really milk this situation for all it was worth.

He went up to the bathhouse and knocked on the door and said in an old womanly voice, "Room service."

Emmi laughed and spoke through the door, "Could you kindly tell Roderick if you see him that we are waiting for our cloaks?"

Roderick, pretending to be an old servant, "I'll see if I can find him Miss." Then he made stepping sounds with his feet and said "I think I hear him coming Miss."

Roderick then cleared his throat, speaking in a deep manly tone, "This is the noble Roderick at your service."

The Princess now answered, preturbed, "Roderick, we are freezing in here, hand us our cloaks please."

Roderick didn't want to them get off that easily, "Only if I receive something in return from a special blonde lady named Emily Anne Sika."

Emmi burned with light revenge, he knew that she hated her full name. She knew that Roderick was going to have to pay for that. Emmi answered, "Sir, you have been most kind to us, pray tell what token would you like? Perhaps a shoelace from my shoe?"

Roderick knew that she was messing around with him. He liked that she had a sense of humor. "My lady, I was thinking about something from your lips."

Emmi answered, "I will discuss with the Princess and return my answer." Then they had some hushed whispering. Then a moment later, Emmi answered while slightly opening the door and letting her hand out. "Kind sir, if you were to hand us our cloaks, then I promise that you shall receive something from my lips."

Roderick laughed and handed her the two cloaks. After a minute or two, the Prince came around the bend, looked at Roderick and said dryly, "Women, even while they are only wearing simple traveling cloaks, still take forever."

Roderick scratched his chin, "I couldn't agree more."

Then the ladies emerged from the bathhouse. They were not dressed like from the ball. They had no makeup, and no jewelry. Even without all the fanfare and glitter, the ladies looked beautiful and radiant.

The Prince bowed and kissed the bare hand of the Princess. "Isabella, I have never seen you more beautiful." The Princess blushed.

Roderick definitely didn't want to be upstaged, so he took the hand of Emmi and twirled her around and waltz with her in his arms. He whispered in her ear, "Just let me know when I deserve something from your lips."

Emmi pulled away and smiled, "You didn't think I would be that easy did you? Besides I told you never to use my full name. How about a rain check for later?"

Roderick heart fluttered with anticipation and he rolled his eyes. "Oh women!"

After Roderick had washed his face and hands, everyone walked down through the warehouse door and into the large field. Their spirits were high. The sun was setting low on the horizon.

The Prince turned to Roderick, slapping him on the back, "So Roderick, what is the plan?"

Roderick liked being the one in charge, it came easily to him. He felt at his side for the bag of farthings. "Well your highness, we must first eat."

The Prince and the Princess looked at each other and said, "Now he is speaking our language."

Emmi laughed and reached for Roderick's hand. They were definitely the oddest pair of travelers that she had ever seen.

-- -- -- -- -- --

Áron and I were almost ready to go. We looked at each other and laughed. We looked awful, literally. Áron blackened one of his beautiful front teeth with soot. His morning scruff had turned to night scruff on his face with a little coal. He powdered his beard and hair to give his thirty years. He put straw and pieces of mud in his hair to mess it up. He arched his back forward and leaned on an old cane.

I didn't look much better. I put cotton pillows in my dress and wrapped it with rope. It was actually hard to breathe and walk while wearing an extra thirty pounds. I knew from that moment that I would never want to get to that point. I didn't know how the royals did it. I also put powder in my hair and put on an old pair of reading spectacles down on my nose like my old teachers. Then I found a piece of black torn fabric and wrapped my shoulders around with it.

He looked at me and immediately started laughing. "You look terrible."

I laughed at him, "You don't look so good yourself."

Then we both were in stitches.

Áron could barely stop laughing, "I think that instead of looking like criminals, we just look like poor old people."

I agreed. "How about we lose the powder, the glasses and the canes and we just wear all black and smoke cigarettes and take on some pretty down-and-out accents?"

Áron also agreed, "Sounds like a plan."

I dropped the weight in ten seconds flat, put on one of Emmi's black dresses and tore some of the sides and the bottom. "Sorry about the dress Emmi," I said.

Áron laughed, "She would know that it's for a good cause anyway."

I shook my hair and put some light soot on my face and blackened one of my teeth. I also went and stepped in some pig mud outside to make my boots look worn.

Áron shook out the powder and straighten up his back. He donned a long, black coat and found an old torn bowler hat in the back room. He rubbed some soot on his face and hands. He took the pipe from the evidence and put it in his mouth and stood all gangling and evil.

I saw him and smiled. "Bravo!"

He looked outside his house, "The sun is beginning to set. That means that criminals should be out soon. Let's get the horse and carriage ready."

"Horse and carriage?" I asked.

"Yeah even criminals have a mode of transportation."

-- -- -- -- -- --

Roderick and the others walked around town. They could hear the clanging of beer glasses and the smell of food coming from the local pub.

Roderick had to think of every detail so that they didn't bring attention to one another. Roderick turned to the Prince and Princess, "Sires, we must not act like you all are royalty. We have to get new names as well if anyone asks us. We can't risk having any one being suspicious of us."

The Prince answered, "So, what do you suggest?"

Emmi spoke up, "We can't look like we are really traveling together. We can't even have manners."

The Princess looked disgusted, "Well, the nerve."

Roderick added, "Drop the royal accents too. Wear your hoods and don't make eye contact."

Emmi looked at him, "Roderick, how do you know how to be normal person?"

Roderick laughed thinking of his scum uncles, but not wanting to give himself away he said, "Didn't you know that I am well versed in many cultures? That's part of being the bodyguard of the Prince. We have to blend in everywhere."

Emmi looked surprised and then jabbed him, "Well, after tonight you can add 'lowly criminal' to your resume."

Roderick laughed, loving her dry sense of humor.

Then he reached for the bag of money. Roderick passed out five farthings each. "If anyone asks you who you are and where you are going, just say you all are pilgrims passing through to pay homage to the Prince and the Princess."

The Princess and the Prince looked at each other, "Why would people want to pay homage to us?" Said the Prince.

Roderick cleared his throat, "Apparently because there was a royal announcement posted in all the villages that you both are dead." He decided to leave out the part about their fathers, since that would be sensitive topic.

"Dead," Whispered the Princess. "How could that be? Who would even know?"

"I guess there were spies in the kingdom." Roderick said.

"Well that's a bummer." Said the Prince.

"Remember, act like pilgrims." Emmi said

He thought this was pretty logical. He had seen one or two pilgrims in the market already today. They all wore traveling cloaks like them. Hopefully no one would be able to tell who the real pilgrims were.

The news of the Royals fathers was soon found out when they went to open the door to the pub, they saw there in black and white the notice that have been posted over the kingdom. The travelers read it solemnly. The Prince and the Princess especially hung their heads in mourning and crossed themselves for their fathers. They didn't even have a chance to say goodbye.

Roderick squeezed the Prince's shoulder and Emmi hugged the Princess. But they knew that as soon as they entered the pub, they had to pretend as if nothing had happened. Roderick knew that especially the Princess had to be brave and not give away anything in the little establishment.

Then they entered solemnly one-by-one into the pub to hopefully halfway enjoy a meager dinner. The Prince especially hoped there was something liquid to wash this whole day away.

-- -- -- -- -- --

Áron and I pulled up to another village about twenty minutes away from Áron's house. We had already checked around at Castlegate and there were no signs of criminal hangout spots, like alleys, pubs or old abandoned buildings. Hopefully this village will bring us more luck.

On the way there, I saw something sparkly on the ground. Gold? Silver? I told Áron to pull over. I bent low to the ground and pulled out a torn piece of fabric that had little sparkles in it. I put my hand over my mouth. Áron jumped down to join me. He knew it the minute he saw it. It was from Emmi's dress.

"She was here." Said Áron. "She must have passed by this way during the kidnapping."

The fabric was muddy and worn; it was hard to tell what time of the day that it had been dropped.

I sketched the fabric in my notebook. I looked at it carefully.

"Áron, looked at the way that the fabric is torn. It's not ripped like if she was getting down from a carriage and it accidently got ripped, it looks as if it was torn on purpose."

He took the delicate fabric from my hands and looked at it. "You're right. Why would she tear her dress?"

"I don't know," I said at first. I walked twenty feet over, down the path and I saw another piece.

"Here is another one." I said to Áron.

He walked a little further past me. "I found another. She was making a trail for us to follow." He smiled from ear to ear, so proud of his sister.

We went back to the horse and carriage. We needed to follow the torn fabric, to wherever it would lead.

We *clip-clopped* very slowly down the road. We must have looked ridiculous, stopping every twenty feet or so to pick up something on the ground. People were looking out of their windows, trying to see what we were doing. But we didn't care, we were focused.

The trail took us to an empty lot with a huge empty warehouse. We saw no vehicles parked. We heard no voices. We only saw a few crows coming in and out of flight.

It was eerie and I held on to Áron's arm as we entered the warehouse carefully. The crows *ca-cawed* us as a warning. We entered and the smell was overwhelming. It was manure mixed with pig slop mixed with blood.

Blood.

There was bloodshed. We didn't know by whom or by what. There was straw strewn on the ground in random patterns, as if it had been lying aimlessly for countless months. There were no human bodies on the ground, only a few dead rats. That was definitely a relief to us, knowing that at least if anyone was murdered, the criminals had the decency to bury the slain.

I looked down at the ground; there was a few sparkles and even one of the Princess's earring. I sketched all the findings in my notebook. I spoke to Áron, "They were here." I held up my evidence. "Hopefully no one is injured or at least badly injured. We should walk around the grounds a bit."

As we were walking around, we saw a few foot prints, two sets and then a set of four. They were walking towards a back shed of sorts. We followed the trail. Áron listened carefully at the door to see if anyone was inside. He heard no rustling or voices. He slowly opened the creaking door.

He motioned me inside, "It's just an old bathroom."

I peeked inside and I held my nose in disgust, "An old *nasty* bathroom."

I looked inside the browned ring tub, "There's water on the bottom. That means someone used it today."

I looked through some old rags and found a sparkly necklace buried deep. It was definitely the Princess'.

Áron dug as well and found a very large pair of trousers, sprinkled with blood. He looked at the tag, "Who do we know wears size 52 trousers?"

I could only think of one person in the entire kingdom. "The Prince."

We uncovered two gowns, and the men's outer clothes. But no undergarments, not that I wasn't disgusted to think about finding the Prince's size 52 whitey tighties but after all, it was evidence.

I smiled to myself and said, "So is everyone walking around in their undergarments?"

Áron laughed, "Now that would be a sight, wouldn't it?" Then he went back to serious. Something was on his mind.

Aron saw my puzzled face and looked through my sketches. "So we found some jewelry, some outer garments and the bath tub has been used recently." He looked at the tub, it was filthy, but no blood stains or drips followed outside of the tub or through the door. He pointed to the door, "There is no blood leading out to the door. It seemed that it was all washed away in the tub as they were all bathing. If someone was badly injured, we would have seen torn cloth or make-shift bandages, or even a trail of blood leading out. But there is none."

"Good point." I said, looking at the walls. I looked at the mud prints on the floor. If someone was struggling, there would probably be drag marks on the ground or marks on the wall as well. Clothes would have been cast aside. These clothes seem to be half-way folded and hidden carefully."

Áron spoke, "According to our findings, hopefully our missing persons are clean, dry, half naked and halfway alive. Let's hope they stay that way."

He looked at my face, I had a half-shocked look. He corrected himself, "Hopefully they stay alive, not half naked."

I raised my eyebrows, "I know what you meant. But that would be gross and half way humorous to think about."

We left the bathhouse and followed the footprints to the front fence. There were not fresh carriage marks on the ground, besides our wheel's markings, there was no burial sites or blood. It would have seemed that the four sets of prints just walked out.

12: MEAL WITH CRIMINALS.

We left the warehouse compound confused and a little hopeful. We were still unsure about the dead rats and the torn and bloody clothes.

I knew that now we must find out what happened to everyone. I could tell Áron was bursting from the seams on the inside, but he had to look the part on the outside. He was a brave man.

We had a mission and a plan, to find some bad people, ask some questions, find out about the pipe, find the possible whereabouts of the illusive criminals and then figure out what happened to Emmi and the others.

Áron and I were getting a little hungry as well. They could smell soup coming from a local establishment. Smoke rose from the chimney. It was warm and inviting. The pub was brightest light in the town. The shacks in the village were dreary and brown compared to the little pub. Only a few homes had even a candle.

I had never seen such a poor town. Even growing up in a village near the castle, we were not rich, but we always had candles to light our table. It was almost ghostlike. No one was around, even at dusk. I could see a few old faces peeking out of wooden shudders to see who was clopping into their town.

I felt more awkward then anything. Even though I looked like a regular criminal, I didn't feel like one. I felt scared and unsure. Áron on the other hand was in character of course. He had put the pipe away and had rolled a cigarette. He was chewing on it menacingly. He nodded for me to tie up the horse and to come inside.

We entered, our heads were down. Áron asked for two beers and two bowls of soup without saying a word and laid down ten farthings on the wooden counter. We sat in silence at the counter slurping our soup and wiping our mouths with our sleeves.

The outer door creaked open. I wanted to look who it was, but I looked around at the other customers, they were too involved in playing poker and drinking to pay attention, so I didn't look up.

A large figure sat next to me at the counter and nodded towards my meal. A bowl of soup was slid down the counter as they put down five farthings down. They were lucky to catch the bowl, as it came in fast. The beer was passed a little slower.

I couldn't help but semi pay attention to the person next to me. They weren't eating quickly like a hungry peasant. They were waiting. Waiting for what? It was like they were inspecting their food or something. They held up the large spoon to their eyes, the soup broth dripping into their bowl and then they took a cautious bite.

I was a little curious and wanted to peek at my next door neighbor without wanting to look nosey. I knew that if I was caught drawing too much attention to myself then I wouldn't be a very good criminal. So I just sneaked a peak at the person's hands. Just a short look. The chubbiness, the mole on the left ring finger. It couldn't be!

-- -- -- -- -- --

Áron heard the outer door open and one-by-one four separate people came into the pub. A thin women with a brown hood below her eyes sat next to him. Her hands were delicate and long. She put five farthings down on the table and received a bowl of soup and a beer.

Áron didn't want to be suspicious. He just wanted to be aware of everyone in the room. There was Dozy in the back. There was Poker, Bluff and Aces playing in the corner booth. There was Fatso sitting in the corner eating his soup hungrily. There was Bounty Hunter in the middle seats putting his black muddy boots up on the seat in front of him drinking beer. There was Captain the bartender, who had beady eyes. There was Chubby next to Priscilla. And then there was Young Lady next to him.

Captain was an old man, probably in his late seventies. He looked old, but he looked sharp as a tack. Like one wrong look or something fishy would send this guy on you faster than a snake on a mouse. Áron knew he had to be careful. He wanted to look around and try to ask some questions, without trying to look as if he was asking questions.

Áron was eating some soup, it was earthy and rich. The girl next to him was eating it as well, but not as fast as him. It was like she was trying to eat around something in the bowl. She ate quietly and calmly. Her little spoon made little *ching* noises as she was eating. Áron was curious. Áron looked in his bowl of soup. The usual, carrots, potatoes, tomatoes, celery and garlic spices were floating around. It was a good hearty bowl of soup.

The girl next to him was done with her soup and got up to leave. Bounty Hunter darted his eyes towards the girl, but made no movements. Áron looked quickly in her bowl. There were about five small bits of soupy tomatoes on the bottom.

Áron got a little pang in his heart. He knew that Emmi was one of the only people he knew that hated tomatoes, which was funny living on a farm where tomatoes grew in abundance. Even mom would also force her to eat them, to no avail. She was one stubborn girl.

Priscilla was elbowing Áron and motioning to go outside. He didn't know why she wanted to leave so early. But he knew that this was Priscilla's way of getting him to go outside to discuss something. Priscilla was quick. He could give her that.

They both nodded to Captain and left the pub. Outside the air was crisp and cool. They got to the carriage and climbed aboard. Priscilla whispered in his ear, "I know that this sounds insane, but I think I saw the Princess."

Áron's brow furrowed. *How could that be? The Prince and the Princess were dead.* Áron looked around to see if there was anyone else around. He answered back, "I did see some interesting people there myself." Aron looked around in the dusk to see in anyone was listening to his conversation. " I really wanted to ask questions, but the bartender looked sharp." Áron's eyes darted back and forth, "There were too many people there to really talk to him alone."

Priscilla whispered back, "What interesting people did you see?"

Áron whispered, "The girl next to me didn't eat her tomatoes."

Priscilla rolled her eyes and sighed. "What?" Asked Áron. It reminded me of my sister who does the same thing."

Priscilla hid a sarcastic laugh, "You mean to tell me that out of all the creepy people in there, the only person that you remember was a young girl that didn't eat her tomatoes?"

Áron started speaking, "Well there was those guys playing poker..."

And then we both felt the carriage move and a small tap on our shoulders. Áron covered my mouth so that I wouldn't scream.

13: THE REALIZATION

Emmi had been gone too long. Roderick knew it. He motioned to the Prince who caught the Princess's eye. They were all to leave one-by-one slowly.

Roderick was the first to leave. He didn't see Emmi outside of the door. He looked around. There was a carriage with two other travelers. The sun was almost gone and the moon was shining bright.

"Psst." He heard from somewhere around the carriage. He looked around

"Psst." It was coming from a mystery person in the carriage.

Roderick was a little afraid. He didn't know the travelers and Emmi was missing. But he had to try to see where that noise was coming from.

He walked slowly over to the carriage. He looked up to the drivers' seats. It was a young lady and a young man. They looked dirty and up to no good, like down-and-out peddlers. The young man was chewing on a cigarette and he spit out his side lip.

Roderick saw a head peep out of the carriage. "Psst." He went to the back to look. It was Emmi.

"What are you doing here?" Roderick whispered desperately. Roderick was about to attack the travelers.

Emmi tried to hide her giggles. "It's Áron and Priscilla!" Emmi pointed up at the carriage seats. Didn't you recognize them?"

Roderick looked up at Áron in the driver's seat. Roderick was so relieved that it was Emmi's brother and not such criminal. He shook Áron's hand and whispered, "Nice you see you chap."

Áron whispered, "Good to see you alive and well as well."

Áron shifted in his seat and took off his hat, "What's going on Roderick?"

Roderick looked around, "No time to explain. This isn't the place."

Roderick looked over at the pub to see the door open. He hid low in the carriage. "When everyone comes out, we all ride together quietly back to a safe place to talk and compare notes."

Áron said quietly, "Sounds good." Then he slunk back into character.

A few minutes later, the Prince quietly sneaks out.

"Psst." Said Roderick.

Priscilla and Emmi both try to hide their laughter as the Prince dumbly looks around to see where the whispers where coming from.

Roderick said, "Hefty, psst."

Prince Gabriel gets the hint and gets in the carriage as fast as his girthy body could manage. Roderick apologizes as he helps the Prince up, "Sorry, I had to use a code name, I didn't want to bring suspicion."

The Prince punched him in the arm, "I'll forgive you this once." The Prince adjusted his cloak and brushed off his shoulders, "Hefty? You make me sound like a big fat guy."

-- -- -- -- -- --

I put my hand over my mouth to stop from laughing at the Prince's remark in the carriage. I thought it was a perfectly appropriate nickname for his large frame.

Then the Princess left the pub. She looks around and sees no one. She looks afraid.

"Psst." Said the Prince.

We all hide their laughter as the Princess looks around to see where the sound was coming from.

"Psst." The Prince said again. "Izzy."

The Princess looked cross and whispered as she struggled to get in the carriage, weighing it down another few inches. She punched the Prince in the arm, "You know I hate that name."

Now Emmi and Roderick are trying to hide their giggles. I look up at Áron, he was beaming with excitement.

Áron taps the horse and whispers, "C'mon boy."

Then we ride in silence through the village back to Áron's farm. Everyone was quiet, but excited, knowing that all the lost parties had been found alive and no one was naked.

-- -- -- -- -- --

It was a chilly evening when we pulled up the farm. After Áron closed the gate and helped me down, we all enter the little farm house.

Áron put on some coffee and got out some bread. We were nervously all speaking at once to one another. There was a frenzy of voices, excitedly telling different bits of stories to each other. Roderick calms everyone down.

Áron motioned to let Roderick speak first. He began his story,

"Emmi and I were walking down the gate the night of the ball and then there was fireworks."

I make little smoochy lips to Aron behind their back, He rolls his eyes.

Roderick could see that I was making fun of him and gives me a look and continues, "The fireworks were brilliant. In all the noises and the lights, all the guards were preoccupied and all of sudden, Emmi feels a blade at her throat."

I looked at Emmi, she puts up a hand to her delicate throat and looks scared.

Roderick continues, "Someone gags us and grabs my keys and throws us in a carriage. "

Emmi interrupted, "I guess the men thought that Roderick and I were the Prince and the Princess or something. Or maybe they just wanted the keys to open the gate. We don't know."

The Princess whispered under her breath, "My villagers don't even know what the Princess looks like! Shameful, uneducated ruffians."

The Prince spoke next, "Well, Isabella and I were enjoying the evening as well. We were watching the beautiful fireworks, when all of all sudden, we were gagged and taken to the same carriage as Roderick and Emmi. "

The Princess shyly added, "We were both a little tipsy then, so we don't know all the details of course."

Roderick smirks, "A little?"

The Princess looks at him and glairs, "We were both a *little* tipsy and did not realize what was happening. We were sleeping pretty much all the way through the carriage ride."

Roderick continued, "Anyways, when we arrived at our location, we were all held inside this large warehouse or barn. I wasn't sure what it was. It was filthy though."

The Princess added, "There were disgusting rats everywhere."

Roderick looked down as if he remembered something, "The bad guys came in and said something about their boss just wanting us out of the way. I wasn't really sure what that meant."

I butt in, "So the bad guys, they weren't the masterminds behind everything?"

Roderick spoke up, "No, they definitely wouldn't be the types. They were just henchmen, sent to do the dirty work of someone else." Roderick looked around to see that everyone was waiting for him to continue. "Well, Emmi and I had to think of a plan fast. Since we figured that we were the 'mistakes'of the operation. They probably really wanted the Prince and the Princess, I thought they would try to get rid of us first."

The Princess looked snobbishly in the air and sipped her tea, "Yes, and this is the last time that Emmi plots a scheme to save our lives."

The Prince hits her on the arm, "Isabella."

The Princess recants, “Sorry Emmi, it was a good plan, but I feel as though I will be getting the stench of that day out of my clothes forever.”

I am curious, “Emmi, what was the idea?”

Emmi smiles, “It was to fake everyone’s suicide. We found some rats and killed them and spread the blood all over our clothes. And then we laid down really still until we thought the bad guys were gone.”

Áron spoke up, “What happened next?”

Roderick finished his thought, “They totally bought it. They just opened the door took one look at our disgusting dead-like selves and left. I guess they left to go back to their boss to tell him what had happened.” He took a sip and wiped his mouth and said, “I think my uncles were too cowered to do the jobs themselves.”

Roderick said it and it hit the air like a heavy weight. The Princess coughed. There was dead silence in the room.

14: COMPARING NOTES

Emmi spoke up, "What do you mean, 'Your Uncles?'"

Roderick got up and leaned on the mantel. His shoulders were heavy and weighted. "I didn't want anyone to know that I knew these men. I didn't mean for that slip out." Then he started to cry. "I... I was going to tell you all earlier... but I didn't know how." He wiped his eyes with his sleeve, "I didn't want you to think that I had any part of this terrible scheme." His eyes burned with passion as he faced everyone, "I swear that I had nothing to do with this. I was as much a victim as anyone."

We all looked around at each other. No one said anything. Finally I spoke up, "Roderick, to be honest, we've had our differences growing up. I know that we are very different people. But deep down, I knew that you could never have a truly evil heart. You are a good man."

Roderick looked at me through tear-stained eyes and nodded.

The Prince spoke up, "I have to say something now. Roderick, I have never made this public, but I think it's important now to mention. When my father still reigned as king..." and the Prince and the Princess crossed themselves in respect

After a moment, the Prince continued, "...and when I was in the care of my tutor, my father told me of a boy that would beg outside the gate of the castle."

Roderick hung his head in shame, he especially didn't want Emmi to find out about his humble beginnings. The Prince continued, "Sometimes the guards and the servants would find him sneaking in to steal food. That boy was you."

The Prince stood up to put his hand on Roderick's shoulder, "My father had pity on you. He told me that he remembered one particular day after the guard dragged you into his study and asked what punishment there would be for stealing from the castle. He remembered looking into your eyes."

Roderick looked right at the Prince's eyes, bracing himself for the worst. The Prince smiled, "They were honest and true." Roderick looked relieved.

The Prince squeezed Roderick's shoulder, "My father could always tell the person's character by their eyes. He said yours were pure. He told me that he remembered that day was the day that he told to guards to make a bed for you in our servant's quarters and to learn from my tutor."

Roderick laughed, "Oh Mr. Sandbridge, you were a very interesting man indeed."

I laughed knowing that his tutor was a very interesting man.

The Prince put his cup down, "That was the day that my father took you into the castle. But most importantly, that was the day that he had my tutor adopt you as a son."

Roderick nodded as if he was remembering that day vividly.

The Prince said, "My father knew that you were raised by greedy men who only saw you as an opportunity to get their way, but with the right environment, you would grow up to be a good man."

Emmi put a hand on Roderick's large shoulder, he was not weeping any more, but standing a bit taller and more confident. Emmi looked into his eyes, "Roderick, you have grown up to be that good man."

Rpderick looked at all of our eyes, "I had no idea that all this was going to happen. I swear, I swear."

Áron spoke up for all of us, "We believe you."

We all nodded in agreement.

The Prince spoke up after pouring another cup for himself, "Roderick, this might actually assist us in putting the pieces together of this mystery." The Prince stirred his hot drink with a spoon, " Have you had contact with your uncles before this night?"

Roderick nodded, "Only to throw them my leftover scraps of food at night sometimes. But I haven't really talked to them about anything."

I felt bad for Roderick. How humiliated he must feel right now. He was having to spill his guts in front of everyone. It made me want to say something that I had done wrong so that I could join him in his humiliation. But I didn't want to ruin the moment. *Hmm, so that's what what keeping my mouth shut feels like.*

Roderick hung his head in shame, "I'm so sorry for keeping this from you all. Every time that they would beg for food, I always felt guilty, like I still owed something to them." He gestured his arms out, " I am their nephew after all, they always looked so poor and harmless." He wiped tears from his face, "And I did it to protect you." He pointed toward the Royals.

The Princess spoke up, "What do you mean?"

Roderick said ashamedly, "Even though I had grown up in the palace my whole life, my uncles always had a mental hold on me, putting fear into my life. They told me that if I didn't feed them then they would do something wrong to you both or blackmail the kingdom in some way."

Roderick sighed, "I never knew if they really had the brain power to do that, but I never wanted to risk something to find out what they were going to do." Then the tears started to come again, "That's why a deep part of me, thinks that this is my fault. That if I would have kept up my bargain, then the kingdom would be safe."

Áron spoke up and put his arm around Roderick, "This is not your fault. There is a deeper evil behind this plot then we can imagine." After a moment Áron spoke again, "In your adventure the past couple days, did you find out any information that might be helpful?"

Roderick nodded, "I was trying to buy cloaks for everyone, who was all left behind in the warehouse, waiting for me..."

"...Naked and helpless," The Princess interrupted.

I laughed, not wanting to think about that visual mental image.

Roderick finished his thought, "I found a kind woman in the village who was the daughter of one of your old hatter's," He said pointing to the Princess.

The Princess looked surprised. Roderick spoke again, "She thought I was associated with evil characters who were bribing her family with these golden royal coins." He opened up his hand to reveal six coins. "I found these in the back room of the warehouse, where my uncle's bathhouse and hideout was."

The Princess fanned herself, "A very disgusting bath indeed. It hadn't been cleaned in a millennium."

Emmi laughed and held her finger to her nose.

I looked at Áron, and started taking notes again in my notebook.

Roderick cleared his throat.

"Well, anyways, the woman refused to give me anything with those gold coins because she didn't want her husband to be any more suspicious than he already was. She made toys and hat for the village. She also said that her and husband had a few whittling jobs from some shady men."

I held up the pipe, "Like this?"

Roderick looked relieved, "My uncle Haggle's lucky pipe. Where did you find this?"

Áron spoke, "In some bushes in the castle."

Then he waved on to Roderick to continue, "Wait, before we get off track, finish your thought about the lady."

Roderick nodded, "She said that she was a good honest woman that didn't want any trouble with her family. Then I told her about my quest and the trouble that we had been having getting food and clothes. She looked at me long and hard and asked a silly question to see if I was telling the truth."

"What was it?" I said.

"What color is the throne room?" Roderick replied.

"Odd question indeed." Said the Prince.

"Well, in her mind, only a servant of the crown would know what the throne room looked like." Said Roderick.

I was puzzled, "How would she know?"

"As a little girl, her and her father visited the palace to present the king with some new hats. They entered the white throne room and the memory was so vivid to her that even now as an old woman, she remembered it."

The Princess spoke up, "And I wanted to change it to something else. Hmm, I think I will keep it white still."

Roderick pulled out a small leather sack, "The old woman asked me to remember her and her family when we retake the throne because of her kindness. She gave me this bag filled with an entire day's wage of farthings. She said that if we used royal gold coins, people would ask questions and get suspicious of us."

I marveled, "She was a good woman. A day's wage is a lot of money for a poor family."

Áron spoke up, "Roderick, you bring up an excellent point. What are we going to do about retaking the throne?"

"I am not sure yet." Roderick scratched his face, "I need more information." There was a pause and then Roderick spoke up again, "Priscilla, Áron, you both should go and tell us about your side of the story."

Áron nodded at me. I rolled my eyes, knowing that I always got to be first, even though I probably would be happier to just sitting back and observing.

I began. "After you all disappeared from the Castle, the Head Council Member, Bishop Sharp, called me and Áron to his audience. He said that he was concerned about your whereabouts and didn't want to alert the kingdom until all the facts were given. So he sent Áron and me away to investigate and try to find you all before the kingdom knew anything."

The Prince spoke up, "That's odd, because as of yesterday, we are dead, according to the postings all over the villages."

The Princess hung her head, "And our fathers."

The Prince and the Princess crossed themselves for the sake of their deceased fathers.

I continued, "I thought that was odd myself. Bishop Sharp specifically told us not to bring attention to ourselves and make people suspicious and start spreading lies about the death of the royals."

Áron interrupted, "At first, we found no evidence around the castle, as if everything had been swept clean, and then we found the pipe."

He handed it to Roderick. Roderick smirked, "My uncle Haggle was very superstitious, always talking about this pipe like a good luck charm." Roderick held it up to the candle light, looking at the letter "H." "He says that he keeps him safe while he does his dirty work. He would say, 'Keeps the ghosts away m'boy.'"

I wrote that quote down in my notebook, along with other important facts from this conversation.

Áron nodded, "Anyways, we started walking around town, trying to find some shady character to talk to, but with Priscilla and I, not looking very criminal like, it was very difficult."

I laughed, "Then we thought of this hare-brained scheme to dress like a bunch of criminals and go to some dark pub in the middle of the night and try to find someone to talk to."

Áron laughed too, "At first we just looked like a bunch of old people and then we changed."

Emmi looked at my dress, "I thought that dress looked familiar."

"Sorry," I said.

Emmi smiled and shook her head, "It's okay, I never liked that dress anyway."

Áron pointed at Emmi, "But in our adventures, all we found was my sister, who took us hostage in our own carriage."

Emmi smiled and nodded, "Yeah, some criminals you turned out to be."

Áron looked curiously at Roderick, "Tell us more about your uncles, did they ever tell you what jobs they did?"

Roderick took a sip of tea, "Scum work. You know, stealing sheep, framing innocent people, making people talk, that sort of stuff. Not murdering people or killing babies or anything senseless. Nothing really like this. They were both too stupid to get into something like this." Then Roderick hesitated, "Unless there was a huge reward available."

Roderick continued, "I usually tried not to listen to their stupid stories, I didn't want any part of their lives anymore. I just wanted to give them the food and get out of there. But every year they always told me their most haunting job story. The job that would make them afraid of ghosts forever. They usually told the story to me every year on Halloween. It really gave me the creeps."

Áron said, "What was it?"

"My uncles were told by their boss, whoever he was, that there was a family that was getting too big headed and needed to be humbled a little bit. They said that the boss told them not to kill anybody, just kill a few sheep or so. No big deal. My uncles told me that they would remember that night for the rest of their lives.

They thought the family was away, they didn't see anyone around or any lights on. The carriage was gone. So they set fire to the barn. They said that they never would forget the way the lady screamed as she was locked in the barn with the flames." Roderick shuddered, and then he looked at me. I was pure white.

15: LAVENDER AND EARTH

I dashed through the cottage door with tears streaming down my face. The only lights shining were the candles lit across the street at the market and the full moon above me.

I ran up the front gate. It was intermixed with old and new wood, as if Áron had just fixed up the previous owners broken down fence.

I sat down in the cold earth, my hands covering my weeping face. I cried and wailed, laying my head against the old fence.

My memory flashed to my old farm, my father tall and strong, my mother laughing and throwing hay at me in the barn. My mother and I watching chicks grow up from eggs to full grown chickens.

Some memories were very vivid to me. One particular memory reminded me of today. When I was a kid, I was allowed to keep one chicken after my parents sold the others at market for a good price. My little chicken was a little brownish red hen. I loved her so much. I named her Henny. And she was my best friend, after Marksman, the horse, of course.

Then one day back from shopping with dad, I went to check on my little chicken in the barn. My chicken was gone. I remember running to my mom and telling her that my chicken was gone when all of a sudden I saw her pull a whole chicken out of the oven.

I was as devastated as an eight year old could be. Henny was my pet! How could they do this to me? I remember my dad told me that when times got tough for the family that Henny would have to "take one for the team." But I never thought they meant it.

I remembered that I ran to a fence, one very similar to this one and I wept, leaning my head against the fence. I remember the smell of something very strong next to my head. It was lavender. My mother grew it all over our fences, up and down. The purple bells drip-dropping over the fences in the spring time. It was a beautiful sight to behold.

I even remember her etching our names in the fence, right near the front gate saying that that spot, where the lavender grew the most, was our special family spot.

I remembered the rich lavender smell as I sat and wept, devastated as an eight year old could be. My father came over to me and put his arm around me and just held me. I could smell the earth of his shirt and the deep, rich sheep smell on his boots. Some people would have thought that a sheep farmer stunk, but not me. I loved the dark, musky smell.

My memory faded. *It was all Roderick's uncles' fault that I couldn't hold my father again. How did I ever know? Did Roderick ever purposely hide it from me?*

I wept, grabbing hold of the fence, using it to support my shaking. My hands tightened around the old moist wood. I felt the grains of the old wood, swirling and worn. But then I felt odd shapes in the fence. It wasn't nail holes, it wasn't swirls, and it was something else.

Áron was running toward me with a lantern. I could see that he was panicked, not knowing what I would do next.

He came near and took my hand and held up the lantern to see my tear stained face. I looked over to the fence, scraping away grime and dirt that were covering up a worn carving of letters.

H. E. A.

R. W. A.

P. L. A.

Áron squinted and looked with me, "What do they mean?"

I replied, closing my eyes, letting their names be said for the last time, "Hannah Emilia Agneu, Rupert William Agneu and Priscilla Louise Agneu."

He paused for a long time, "This was your family."

I nodded and cried again.

Then he hugged me and held me close, I could smell the rich earth of his shirt against my face, almost like my father's smell.

Áron whispered, "I already knew this was your family's farm. I just didn't want to walk up and tell you, that I was living there." He hesitated, "I didn't know if you would approve."

I sat up and looked at him, "You did?"

He put his head down with shame, "I didn't know until you told me how your mom died. I had just moved here from another village and I was looking to buy some new land for my family. I asked around the village and they told me that this farm hadn't been lived in for years. They said that people were afraid to live here because of superstition." He started to cry on my shoulder, "If I would have known you then and known how much your family meant to you, I would have never moved my family here."

I touched his cheek, it was warm and soft, I looked at him so intently. "No, Áron, I think my father would have wanted a man like you to take it over for him."

We just held each other for a while. His hug was deep and strong, just like my father's was. My memory flashed back to the smell of lavender and earth.

I was home again, finally home.

-- -- -- -- -- --

It had been an hour or so since I ran away from the house. Everyone started to slowly come out to see if I was okay. First it was sweet Emmi. Then the Princess and then the Prince. Finally Roderick came, defeated and ashamed.

I wanted to hate him, I wanted to, but I couldn't. He had been a distant friend all those years. Sometimes an he was an annoying guy, sometimes he was the cute guy at the end of the room that I was too afraid to talk to, but he was always there. Past his tough exterior was a little afraid boy, trying to be a better man than his previous examples. I knew that.

When Roderick came, I held out my hand to him and said, "I don't blame you Roderick, this wasn't your fault. You weren't even there." But then I hesitated. "You weren't there, were you?"

He shook his head, he kicked some dirt, "I was at our village stealing food. I remember that night very vividly. My uncles said that they were going to be extra hungry that night, so I needed to steal a chicken or something. I remember that I was only nine or ten, so I didn't know if I could steal a chicken without getting caught, so I just walked up and made myself look pathetic and beg door to door for food." Roderick laughed, "I remember feeling ashamed that I never could be the thieves that my uncles were." He laughed a dry laugh.

Emmi took Roderick's hand. And she put her head on his shoulder. The Prince put his arm around the Princess. We all sat in silence, listening to the sounds of the night when Emmi spoke up and held Roderick close, "Let's go back inside before anyone gets suspicious about six adults crying and chatting outside in the middle of the night."

We all agreed. We all went back to the cottage. Áron put another log on the fire and started chopping up potatoes for a late-night snack.

It was a very awkward time for us, sitting around, not knowing what someone would say to make me cry again. It had been rough couple days. Our Kings were dead. The Princess and Prince died, and then were resurrected, Emmi and Roderick went missing and then turned up later, I found out who killed my mom.

The crackling fire was keeping us from exploding from the silence. Everyone's faces were concentrated and solemn. Even my sarcastic humor couldn't immediately heal the pressure that we were all feeling.

I spoke up, knowing that it was I alone that could break the silence, "Well, here we all are. They tried to kill you all, but couldn't. They tried to discourage Áron and I, and they failed. I can only imagine the plans that they have for us when they find out that we are all still alive and well."

Everyone's eyes looked hopeful, as If I was giving a speech to a bunch of discouraged polo players. So I began again, "This is what I think. I think we should use our experience and our common knowledge to find a way to get to the real mastermind behind this scheme. "

The Princess spoke up, "Who you do you think that is?"

Roderick cut in, "I believe it has to do with someone inside the palace, like a Council member. Only someone like that can pay their people in royal gold coins."

The Prince spoke up, "That's correct Roderick. But who would want the Princess and me out of the picture?"

I spoke up, "Someone like Bishop Sharp."

Roderick knodded, "Bishop Sharp, the leader of the Council that could legally rule until the law of St. Beatrice was acted upon."

Emmi looked confused, "I am not familiar with this kingdom's rules."

The Prince spoke strong and confident, "The Law of St. Beatrice was made in case of an emergency in the kingdom. When, God forbid, the King and the Queen or the Prince and the Princess were dead and there were no heirs in line, then the Council would be able to rule. They would be able to rule until a time where they would call for an election to a valiant man or woman to be the new elected King or Queen. We have never had this happen in our kingdom before. There has always been heirs to take over the kingdom."

Áron checked the potatoes from the oven and spoke up, "Except in this case."

I said, "That's right, your majesties' parents have all passed..."

Everyone paused and crossed themselves in a moment of respect.

Priscilla continued, "Also, your majesties are newlyweds and haven't made an heir yet."

The Princess blushed and looked at the Prince, who raised his eyebrows to her and winked. As if to say he that he would be happy to make one as soon as this whole fiasco is over.

Emmi said, "So right now, the only way for another ruler to rule is for the Council to let go of their power and make a royal announcement that an election will happen."

Yeah, I knew that wasn't going to happen, and I said, "That's definitely not going to happen unless we storm the castle or something and steal the royal Council's seal. And after we survive that, then we make an election ourselves."

I was laughing now. What a sight that would be, all of us, unseen, sneaking past all the castle's guards and soldiers and magically appearing in front of the mastermind of this whole plot. I was howling now, thinking about all six of us against the Council members and the criminal cronies and them just handing the ring over just like that. I laughed, wiping the tears from my eyes. I saw that the Prince and the Princess were chuckling with me. But Roderick's faith was determined like a flint.

Roderick was looking at me intently and said, "That's exactly what we are going to do."

16: LINENS DAY

Mrs. Cuire knew that something was brewing today and it wasn't just her pot of morning coffee that was wafting in from the kitchen. Something was happening.

Kai was helping kneading dough for some morning bread with some other ladies. Mrs. Cuire looked at her and nodded her head in one direction as if to say, "I need to speak with you."

Kai wasn't usually quick when it came to subliminal messages, but today by some stroke of genius, she understood Mrs. Cuire hidden sign.

Mrs. Cuire pulled Kai aside and wiped her cook's hands with a moist towel, "Kai, I can feel something happening." Kai listened intently. Her eyes were fixed on Mrs. Cuire's. "It's been two days since your brother and Priscilla were asked to go investigate the missing Prince and Princess. I am beginning to think that something else has happened to them."

Kai nodded, knowingly, "What do you want me to do?"

"I want you to take a carriage and go to your farm. If anyone asks; you are going to get a pig for tonight's dinner. I want you to ask around the village to see if anyone has seen them or if there are any clues in the house."

Timothy walked by, dressed in his usually guard uniform, full coat of mail and armor. Mrs. Cuire could hear his *clink-clink* coming in from a mile away.

Mrs. Cuire, pulled him into their secret meeting. His armor *clanged* and then Mrs. Cuire banged a pot together to hide his sound.

"Mrs. Cuire," Timothy stammered, looking frightened, "I didn't steal any muffins today, I swear."

Mrs. Cuire hid a laugh, "Have you stolen some muffins from me before Timothy?"

Timothy lowered his head, "Yes ma'am. They are just so fresh, I couldn't help myself."

Mrs. Cuire rolled her eyes, "I already knew you have been stealing them from me. You always leave a trail of crumbs in your mail shirt."

Kai snickered at Timothy's predicament and looked up at him smiling.

Timothy blushed. Mrs. Cuire pulled him in closer and whispered, "That's not the reason I pulled you in right now, I need you to escort Miss Kai home to fetch a pig for tonight's supper. I don't want a pretty lady like herself going out to town all alone."

Timothy smiled and saluted, "No ma'am, absolutely not, not a pre-pretty girl like Miss Kai." He stammered.

Mrs. Cuire laughed, "At ease Private. Just keep an eye on her today."

Timothy reached for Kai's hand, "Oh yes ma'am, much obliged to do so ma'am."

Kai blushed and saw Mrs. Cuire wink at her as she left the little secret pantry.

Timothy was about to leave, but Kai reached up and kissed him on his cheek.

Timothy stood there for a second and then he touched his cheek. Oh he was definitely smitten now. *Back to work,* he thought. Then Timothy clanged again as he stepped back into his position, he put his helmet back on, so that Kai's kiss on his cheek wouldn't be seen. How unprofessional.

-- -- -- -- -- --

It was an early morning for everyone at Áron's house. We ate some bacon with potatoes and fresh eggs from the chicken coop. I was feeling more and more at home here with Áron. I was up at five milking the poor overlooked cow. I then gathered eggs with Áron by my side. I had forgotten how much a farm needed constant attention. But I didn't mind at all. Afterwards, I went to the kitchen to start cooking.

Through the small window, I could see Áron, Roderick and the Prince, of course in a disguise, catching a poor pig for our morning's breakfast.

Emmi, the Princess and I were all peeling potatoes and making eggs. The Princess had never pealed a potato before. Emmi and I both had a good laugh looking at her carefully trying to peel the potato without getting any pieces on her hands. We both peeled about five each before the Princess had finished one. But we all smiled and shared a funny moment together.

Our plan for the day was somewhat put together. We knew what we would do when we would get inside the castle and inside the Council's chambers, but we hadn't quite worked out what we were going to do to get into the castle. Nobody had any good solid ideas. Roderick suggested a good breakfast in the morning and some brainstorming time would be very helpful for us. Of course, the starving Prince and Princess couldn't agree more.

After seconds and thirds from the royals, we heard a familiar sound of a carriage coming up the dirt path right to Áron's house.

I looked through the window; it was the kitchen's carriage, the one used to pick up groceries from the market. I knew it well. I motioned for everyone to stay down. I couldn't make out the drivers to see who was coming up to the house.

I saw the mail shirt, "It's a guard!" I whispered.

Roderick sat up and headed for the door, "I can take him. If they've come to arrest us, he won't even know what hit him!"

I saw a blonde woman, "Wait Roderick! It's Kai and.... I think that's Timothy."

Áron sighed, "It's just Kai. She's probably coming to check on the pigs or feed the chickens."

Emmi huffed, "I would be greatly surprised if that lazy bum came up with that idea herself."

Áron playfully punched her in the arm, "Emmi, that's mean. Kai is growing into a mature young lady."

Emmi looked at him suspiciously, "Hmm mmm." She hummed.

I slightly cracked open the door and waved the two inside and made a shushing face with her finger.

They both snuck inside after tying up the horse.

Kai entered first and saw Priscilla and Áron at the sink, washing dishes, then she saw Emmi and Roderick ducking behind their little wooden rocking chairs and then she saw the Prince and the Princess sitting on little wooden stools.

She nearly screamed out loud in excitement, but Timothy covered her mouth. I gave thumbs up to Timothy. "Good thinking, we wouldn't want her to give away our little hiding spot."

I looked over to Áron, who was putting all the leftovers on a plate. "Why don't we get some breakfast for our guests as we explain everything?"

Kai sat down at a bench with Timothy, "That sounds like a good idea, because I am really confused."

-- -- -- -- -- --

It was almost lunch time when Timothy cantered the horses into the service gate of the palace. The guards saw Kai and tipped their hats. They saw the kitchen's covered wagon with a large fat pig and a few smaller pigs hanging out the back.

One guard laughed. "It looks as if we are having some pig tonight."

They waved them through to the back of the castle to where the kitchen entrance was.

Kai entered first and got Mrs. Cuire, who was delighted to hear about the plan. Mrs. Cuire got the pigs out and rolled in some large laundry baskets to the side of the wagon. Timothy bribed any watching guards with some of the fresh cookies from the oven while six people got into six different laundry baskets.

The laundry baskets were taken inside the castle. Kai threw a few linens and table cloths in each basket. She knew that she couldn't wheel them all herself, so she called two other maids to help. Today was linens day anyway so no one would be the wiser.

Kai and the two maids pushed the wheeled baskets up the elevators; they were the heaviest baskets that they had ever pushed.

The maids looked exhausted as they took the elevator to the top floor.

One spoke up, "What's in these things, rocks?"

Kai laughed, "Mrs. Cuire wanted us to do all the table cloths, sheets and pillow cases in the castle today for some reason, something about spring cleaning or whatever."

Another maid wiped her forehead, "I hate that women's 'Spring Cleaning' she had me pulling out hair from all the tub drains last year. That was the worst." Then she started laughing, well at least it wasn't as bad as Priscilla's job."

One of the basket's coughed and Kai sneezed to cover up.

The maids both said "Bless you" as the elevator dinged open.

Kai whispered to my basket, "That was close."

All six laundry baskets were placed outside of the Council's chamber door.

Kai thanked her friends and told them "Other maids would be helping me bring all of these baskets down to the laundry room."

The maids looked relieved and left.

Six heads poked out of six smelly laundry baskets. While the coast was clear, six people silently climbed out of six laundry baskets and gathered around the Council's chamber door. Áron whispered to Priscilla, "What was your spring cleaning job last year?"

Priscilla rolled her eyes, "Unclogging all the royal septic tanks."

Áron hid a laugh.

Roderick motioned for all of them to hush. He leaned into the Council's door. There was whispering and hushed tones coming from the large oak door. There were only three people in the room and Roderick knew exactly who two of them were.

-- -- -- -- -- --

I was so grateful to get out of that basket, it smelled like rotten tomato soup and bed pans. I had not realized that taking the service elevator up ten floors would make me feel so nauseated. I laughed to myself thinking about how the Prince and the Princess were doing in their smelly damp laundry baskets. I could just see the Princess' face now. I am sure that it was feeling as green as the stains on the table cloths.

I could see Roderick listening into the door. I freshened up my makeup and the applied some powder to the Prince and the Princess' face. We had rehearsed this all last night, so I knew that we were ready. But the question that we were all wondering was "Was this going to work?"

We sure hope it did, if not, then we were in a load of trouble. *Ha ha, "load," of trouble. That's funny considering we just came out of laundry baskets. Priscilla, concentrate, stop trying to be funny!*

The plan was for me to go first. *Why did I have to go first? Couldn't we all just go all together? I guess this goes back to my theory of always getting the dirty jobs.* Áron gave me thumbs up for good luck. At least he believed in me.

Roderick pushed the door wide open and I slinked into action.

My white robe was covering my white face. My hands covered in tomato sauce. My clothes covered in burn marks from the fire, I screamed and wailed, "You! You did this to me!" I pointed a ghastly bloody finger at one goonie. I could see that he looked as scared as I was scary. "I was milking my cow in my barn and then there were flames! Terrible flames!" My voice went into a ghoulish sing-song tone.

One of goonie's face turned white and he screamed, "The lady form my dream! She has come back to get her revenge!"

Roderick and Emmi entered, holding their stomachs covered in fake blood. They looked ghastly. Roderick looked at his uncles' frightened eyes and snarls, "Uncles, you would even kill of your own nephew?"

One goonie hits another and said, "I told you Smith not to kill him."

The other goonie clutches his brother, "Now they've come for us!"

Then the Princess slinks into the stage, blood all over her clothes, a knife in her armpit. "You all killed me!" She points to Bishop Sharp and pulls the knife out of her bloody armpit. She waves the knife at him with a zombie-like shaking hand.

The three men looked horrified.

She was good. I could tell that this was working. We were inching in on them, slowly and slowly closer to the large window. Even Bishop Sharp looked squeamish.

The Bishop cried out, "Your Majesty? We thought you were dead!"

Then the Prince came into view, dragging a zombie leg and grabbing the Bishop by the throat, his breathy voice whispering over him, "We were! But we come from the grave to seek our vengeance!"

Both goonies jump out of the window at this point. The Bishop was getting close to the exit, his face pure white, his hands were around his neck, trying to stop the Prince from taking his life.

Then the Princess walked a zombie walk toward him. The Prince was snarling and drooling bloody slime, "You also killed our fathers! You will pay for your crimes!"

Bishop Sharp squeaked, "No they died of broken hearts! I swear! When they heard the news of your majesties passing, they both had heart attacks."

The royals press in on him, "It was still your fault," they say, clutching his throat.

The Princess grabs the royal seal off his finger and then pushes him over the edge.

We all looked down the window; it was a two hundred foot drop. No way could they have survived the fall.

After the room was empty, Áron and Kai appear clapping. “Bravo, good show your Majesties. Wow that even scared me a little bit.”

Mrs. Cuire peaked into the large room, she was all smiles. Even timothy came up the elevator, wiping muffin crumbs off of his shirt.

Áron hugged me, knowing that this was the hardest job that I’ve ever been asked to do, and this time I was thanked for it.

The Prince and the Princess smiled and looked a little embarrassed at each other. Then they laughed. They smelled of pig feed, animal droppings, tomato sauce and old sheets.

Everyone hugged and held each other for a long time. We had done it. We had pulled together and not only saved the missing persons, but saved the kingdom.

Emmi pulled Roderick close and gave him a soft and tender kiss. Roderick looked as if he was going to fall over. Emmi spoke, while she held his face in his hands, “I owed you something from my lips.”

Roderick kissed her again and then said, “That was definitely worth the wait.”

I laughed because we looked ridiculous, covered in flour and tomato sauce. It was like we got in a fight with a bag of flour and ketchup and the pantry items won. But everyone laughed and enjoyed the moment.

Everyone deserved a nice long bath. And Áron couldn’t wait, because finally he was getting what he always wanted. And this time, he was going to make sure that nothing, or no one interrupted him.

-- -- -- -- -- --

Gabriel and Isabella were happy that their plan had worked. They were grateful that they could get rid of the evil that had been plaguing their kingdom. However, they needed to do something before anything else could be accomplished. They had to find the burial sites for their fathers and say goodbye for the last time.

17: JUST VISITING

The bell rang me from my sleep. But I ignored it. Because the annoying little gold bell and it's annoying little ring wasn't for me anymore. It was for the new lady in waiting. I was just a guest at the palace now. Just the way I liked it.

This year was a very busy year. With the help of the Council's royal seal, an announcement was made throughout the kingdom to attend a royal ceremony. The Prince and the Princess gave up their crown in front of the entire kingdom. Then at the conclusion of telling the deeds and the adventures of the royals, the people voted Roderick and Emmi their new King and Queen because of their bravery and wisdom.

Of course, unbeknownst to the brave Roderick, I knew that all the young women in the kingdom voted unanimously for him just because they thought he was gorgeous, but of course, I wouldn't want to burst his bubble.

Emmi was a beautiful and brilliant queen. She ruled the kingdom with gentleness and wisdom. She also knew that she could never leave Roderick alone for more than ten minutes, or a riot of female fans might try to maul him.

Roderick was the bravest, most humble and most handsome king that the people and his fan had ever known and he knew it. But as soon as Emmi gave him a look, he knew his place.

In a great celebration of the new royals, there was a double wedding with, Roderick and Emmi and Áron and I.

The party lasted for over two weeks and the whole kingdom rejoiced. Of course there as so much food that the former prince and princess ate to their hearts content, and gained another twenty pounds, which I didn't know was physically possible. But apparently it physically was.

Roderick had invited the townspeople to come and eat at the royal table, including his favorite little old lady who still remembered what color the throne room. She was hired on the spot as the new royal fashion advisor and toy maker. There would soon be babies needing toys in the castle and the little old lady was never so excited to start to get to work.

Now, months after the party, Isabella and Gabriel are enjoying a wonderful quaint life in a private island somewhere where they are honeymooning for a very long time and hopefully making their own heirs.

The bell rings for the third time, waking me out of my day dream. I think to myself, "Kai! That's for you!" I even throw my shoe at the large door as if to say "Shut up!"

I hear Kai running down the hallway. I hear the *clink clang* of a knight chasing after her. Probably Timothy, the Captian of the Guard, that never leaves her side. I laugh at the thought.

I close my eyes and burrow my head in the down pillow that smells like lavender. This bed is much too comfortable, and my husband, much too snuggly for me to want to get out of it. Áron's strong arms hold me close in our fluffy royal bed. Then I drift back asleep.

After a large breakfast with the in-laws we needed to get back home. We were just visiting for the weekend. There were so many things to do at the farm, feed the animals, milk the cows, and make potato and cabbage soup for dinner. I never could be happier.

ABOUT THE AUTHOR:

Christal Marie Marshall doesn't like coffee, always gets stuck doing the "dirty jobs" like scrubbing the toilet, changing filthy diapers and cleaning up toddler messes.

When she is not doing those things, she loves being outside, eating anything chocolate and loves to dip her feet in beachy waters.

Christal Marshall is also a photographer and a designer in her free time. You can follow her images at: www.marshallartsstudiophotography {dot} com or www.studiomarshallarts{dot}etsy{dot}com

Her other titles include: The Summertime Boy, Seven Letters, Escaping Pharisee, The Guardian, and Waiting for the Sun

She lives in Virginia Beach with her Husband and two children and holds a M.Ed from Lynchburg College.

Made in United States
Orlando, FL
04 April 2024

45458642R00095